MOLLY AND THE INDIAN AGENT

Molly rode into Crowheart to solve a murder, but she was about to get swept up into a war in Wyoming. Pioneer rancher Isaiah Holcomb had been savagely left for dead on his own spread. The whites were quick to blame his killing on young Shoshone warriors who had been threatening to thunder off the nearby reservation and turn their hunting parties into blood raids. Molly was convinced the murder was tied instead to a long-simmering plot by the ruthless Indian agent to drive the Shoshone from their land for his own secret gain. She needed proof though, and would dare to go into the heart of the Shoshone encampment, and all while someone was stalking Molly with a bullet, intending to stop her investigation.

MOLLY AND THE INDIAN AGENT

Stephen Overholser

GUNSMOKE

This hardback edition 2008
by BBC Audiobooks Ltd
by arrangement with
Golden West Literary Agency

ISBN 978 1 405 68199 5

British Library Cataloguing in Publication Data available.

Printed and bound in Great Britain by
Antony Rowe Ltd., Chippenham, Wiltshire

CHAPTER I

Molly's horse shied as lightning flashed out of the dark clouds hanging low over southeastern Wyoming. The big buckskin gelding flicked his ears at a deep rumble of thunder, and by the time Molly crossed the iron bridge over the North Platte River her mount was tossing his head and prancing.

She held a tight rein as drops of water the size of half-dollars splashed over the brim of her Stetson and the shoulders of her light jacket. Wearing a divided riding skirt of blue denim that reached to her boot tops, she was a shapely woman with a trim waist and full breasts, riding straight-backed in the saddle. She had left her slicker behind in Denver, and now rat￵er than seek cover she gambled that she would reach Fort Laramie before the full force of the storm hit.

Molly lost the bet. Just as she topped a rise by a cemetery and drew in sight of empty buildings and a parade ground overgrown with weeds, a bolt of lightning exploded out of the black clouds, followed by deafening thunder. The rain came in wind-driven sheets that lashed against her. Molly let the horse run.

The powerful gelding leaped ahead, bursting into full gallop down the old road toward the fort. Molly leaned over his neck, peering through the slanting rain. A long, two-story barracks loomed ahead, and beyond it she saw a row of officers' quarters lining one side of the parade ground.

Molly straightened up and tugged on the reins, bringing the galloping horse under control. She let him canter along the quadrangle, then guided him under the overhanging roof on the south side of a building that had once been the sutler's store. Woman and horse were soaked.

1

She swung down and stood against the wall, grasping her horse's reins at the bit. More thunder boomed, like close cannon fire, and flashes of lightning were so near that they seemed to pierce her eyes. Rain poured off the near corner of the roof in a small, noisy waterfall, splashing into watery mud below.

In a quarter of an hour the storm broke. The high wind ceased as abruptly as it had begun, and the lashing rain became a gentle sprinkle. Minutes later it stopped altogether. Molly led her horse out to the grass that had been flattened and was now gleaming green. The black clouds had moved to the south, leaving an eerie stillness behind.

Molly took off her soaked Stetson and jacket and hung them over the saddle horn. Pulling out the hairpins that held her long blond hair up, she gave her head a shake. Soft hair cascaded down, framing the delicate features of her face.

She stepped out to the front of the sutler's store and looked across the quadrangle that was ragged with weeds. A tall wooden flagpole, paint peeling, stood in front of the administration building like the spire of some lost civilization. Nearby was a guardhouse and stockade with barred windows, and at the far end of the parade ground Molly saw more cavalry and infantry barracks. All were empty.

This famous fort on the Oregon Trail had been abandoned by the army five years ago, in 1890. All the furnishings, all the doors and windows, all the lumber from stables and horse barns, had been sold at auction. Remaining now was the shell of an outpost of white civilization dating back to the fur trapping days—a fort that had been a stop on the Pony Express and later housed more than seven hundred troops at the height of the Indian campaigns following the Custer massacre of 1876.

The sun shone brightly above the black clouds of the receding storm. Molly felt its warmth seeping through her wet clothes. She took out a small timepiece from her skirt pocket and saw that the hour was a few minutes past one in the afternoon.

I'm on time, she thought. *Where's the general?*

Half an hour later her clothes were nearly dry when she heard drumming hoofbeats. She put on her Stetson and her jacket, and turned to see a military escort ride over the hill by the cemetery.

Behind the eight cavalrymen came a high-wheeled, low-slung carriage pulled by four matched blacks. The vehicle flew a United States flag and a division banner from Fort Robinson, the large military reservation just across the state line in Nebraska.

The mounted patrol halted at the far end of the parade ground, and the driver of the carriage drew the team of black horses to a stop behind them. An orderly wearing a slicker jumped down from the seat and moved smartly back to the carriage door.

Molly saw the cavalrymen look around cautiously, glancing at one another as though struck dumb by the sight of this vacant fort. *Ghostly* was the thought that came to Molly's mind while she had waited, and now flesh and blood soldiers in full uniform seemed as though they had somehow ridden out of the past.

The orderly opened the carriage door. General Zachary Monroe Holcomb climbed out. Straightening up slowly, he glanced around until his gaze met Molly's across the quadrangle. Then he gave a terse command that drifted through the empty space, and Molly watched him come toward her, alone.

"Delayed by the storm," General Holcomb said when he was still several paces away.

More an observation than an apology, Molly was surprised that he offered any explanation at all. He was a man with a reputation that was legendary in the West. Known as an iron-willed commander who had driven infantrymen beyond exhaustion in pursuit of Indians, General Holcomb was always at the head of his column, tolerating neither complaints nor excuses from his subordinates.

Now Molly saw that age had caught him. Moving with the stiff-legged walk of an old man, the skin of his craggy face under his hat brim looked like a thin, pale membrane covering dark veins. Brass buttons shone dully on his blue coat, gold braid circled his campaign hat, and as he stopped Molly saw that his black boots were spotted with mud and gleaming droplets of water from his walk across the old parade ground.

"That was some shower," Molly said.

Holcomb grunted at her understatement, then turned and looked at the vacant buildings of Fort Laramie. "We never should have left this one," he murmured.

A long moment passed while his gaze traveled from the administration building to HQ, from the famous officers' quarters known as Old Bedlam to the long buildings that had housed enlisted men. On the hill beyond was the post hospital. While the man's hardened expression revealed none of his thoughts, Molly knew this place must have brought back a flood of memories. Holcomb had served here through the Indian campaigns, and later had been post commander before being shipped to Fort Robinson.

He abruptly swung his gaze back to her. "In my time a woman either managed the hired help, or she was the hired help. I don't like the idea of a woman doing a man's job."

"So I've been warned," Molly said with a smile.

Back in Denver she had received the Fenton Investigative Agency file for this case. It had been delivered by courier from the train station to Mrs. Boatwright's Boarding House for Ladies. Molly had taken the confidential file to her room on the second floor of the converted mansion, locked her door, and began reading.

In a cover letter Horace Fenton explained that it had taken several telegrams between New York City and Fort Robinson to convince General Holcomb that she was the right operative for this assignment. In the beginning Holcomb had wanted three or four gunmen, who could pose as cowhands looking for work.

"He insists on meeting you personally," Fenton wrote, rather apologetically.

Molly carefully read through the file and studied maps to absorb the background of this case. After telegraphing her acceptance to the Fenton office in New York City, she packed her valise and had her horse and gear delivered to Union Station. This was her first big investigative assignment in weeks, and after the dull routine of trailing errant husbands, wives or business partners, she was eager for the challenge.

Molly had ridden the noon passenger train to Cheyenne. After spending the night in the Plains Hotel near the depot, she mounted her horse and rode northeast.

Crossing the high plains toward the North Platte River, she wondered if General Zachary Monroe Holcomb in person was anything like the legendary man of iron portrayed in newspaper accounts. Her thoughts were interrupted by the ominous thunderhead she saw mushrooming in the sky. In her haste to pack she had left her slicker behind.

"Horace Fenton reminded me," General Holcomb said now, "that some of our most productive spies during the Civil War were women, and a woman operative—that is, you—could conduct a thorough, absolutely secret investigation."

Molly acknowledged the point with a nod, even though she did not consider herself a spy. Trained as an investigator, she asked questions and gathered evidence. That was the challenge of her work. The satisfaction was to arrive at the truth. But the distinction between spy and investigator was one the old general might not see, and she did not argue.

"Fenton claims you can look out for yourself if things get rough," Holcomb said. "That true?"

"I can hold my own," Molly replied. She had been schooled by a Japanese master in jujitsu, the art of self-defense, and had been coached to fight with her feet, elbows, and fists.

"You're armed?" Holcomb asked.

Molly nodded, pulling aside her jacket to show the white grips of a nickel-plated Colt Lightning Model .38 revolver in a shoulder holster. With a two-inch barrel, the gun was small enough to be unobtrusive but of a caliber heavy enough to have the stopping power of a larger handgun.

Molly did not show Holcomb the other tools of her trade. Strapped in a holster on her thigh was a two-shot derringer; with her horse was a Winchester repeater in the saddle boot; inside her handbag she carried a set of master skeleton keys and lock probes. In addition, she had been well trained in the art of safe cracking by an ex-convict in New York.

Holcomb drew a deep breath and exhaled, grudgingly acknowledging that she'd come prepared. "Well, as I told your employer," he said, "I'm willing to give this plan a try. That's why I wanted to meet you out here. I never send anyone on a dangerous assignment without talking to him—or her—eyeball-to-eyeball."

He jerked his head toward the mounted soldiers near the carriage across the parade ground. "They think I'm here on some sort of sentimental inspection tour. Rank does have its privileges." He paused. "You've been advised of the secrecy required in this matter?"

Molly nodded.

"No one must know that I'm financing an investigation of civilians," he said. "Plenty of people want me retired out of the army before I'm ready, and if anyone found out about this, they'd have the excuse they've been looking for."

His jaw clenched. "If I wasn't so stove up, I'd resign my commission and do this job myself. But the army's all I've got, and I'm not ready to give up the uniform."

"I never reveal my client's identity without permission," Molly said.

Satisfied, he nodded. "You'll take the train from Cheyenne to Crowheart?"

Molly nodded. "From there I'll ride to the Pitchfork Ranch. I have your map."

"The Pitchfork," Holcomb repeated. "My brother, Isaiah, carved that cattle ranch out of wilderness thirty years ago." Tears welled up in his eyes, and in a voice thick with emotion he went on, "Isaiah's widow, Nell, will be looking for you. She needs help—whether she knows it or not. I want you to look out for her. And I want you to find my brother's murderer."

In that moment of unguarded emotion Molly realized he was not quite the iron man legend made him out to be. The murder of his brother on the Pitchfork Ranch had hit him hard, and left an open wound.

CHAPTER II

Molly's first view of Crowheart, Wyoming, came the next evening as she looked out the window of a passenger coach. The westbound train steamed into a widening valley, following the Wind River. The valley was lush with vegetation. Box elders and cottonwoods lined the clear waters of the river, and grasslands speckled with wildflowers stretched out for miles on either side. Sleek and fat cattle grazed in those pastures.

To the north Molly saw a range of high and rugged peaks capped with snow. They were the Owl Mountains. She had seen them on the map provided by General Holcomb, and knew they were within the boundaries of the Shoshone Indian Reservation.

Frame houses on tree-lined streets appeared as the train slowed. Bell ringing, the engine nosed into the center of town. Crowheart shared its main street, Front Street, with the railroad tracks. Molly saw stores and shops built of brick and stone, or painted board-and-batten. A granite bank stood on a street corner.

Men, women, and children came to watch the weekly passenger train pull in. Molly saw boys in short pants running about, and she smiled as she returned the enthusiastic waves of a group of girls wearing cotton dresses and sunbonnets.

Women on the boardwalks were stylishly dressed in long skirts and blouses with leg-of-mutton sleeves. Their hats were adorned with ribbons and plumes or colorful silk flowers. The men, wearing dark suits or farmer's bib overalls, moved with the train toward the depot.

Molly saw that the Crowheart depot, near the end of Front Street, was a red brick building, steep-roofed to shed the snows of winter. Next door stood another brick structure, a two-story hotel called the Shoshone House. A handsome building with double front doors and all the window frames painted white, it was clearly Crowheart's finest.

Molly climbed down from the passenger coach to a loading platform crowded with people. She made her way through departing passengers and porters to a stock car in front of the red caboose. Her horse was in that stock car, and she hurried back to personally oversee the off-loading. Trainmen generally had little patience with animals.

Molly stopped at the base of the stock ramp leading down from the car's sliding door. She watched as trainmen led half a dozen saddle horses out, and then her own buckskin gelding came down the ramp. She stepped forward and took the reins from a gloved hand of a trainman dressed in greasy overalls.

Molly quickly checked the animal for injuries. Strong and deep-chested, this fine horse had been presented to her by a wealthy gold baron after the successful completion of a difficult case in Cripple Creek, Colorado.

Finding no injuries, Molly hooked her valise over the saddle horn and led her horse away from the train. She was momentarily startled to see a group of still figures standing near the depot building. Eight Shoshone men, having copper-skinned faces with dark eyes and flat noses, stood shoulder to shoulder. They wore high-crowned hats with flat brims, decorated with feathers, and the trousers and flannel shirts of white men. Several women and children stood nearby, bareheaded, with government blankets wrapped around their shoulders. They watched silently but with obvious curiosity at the noisy spectacle created by the coming of the passenger train.

Molly led her horse to the Smythe Livery Barn that she had spotted from the window of the passenger coach. The big unpainted barn stood on a side street, two blocks away from the depot and hotel. At the first corner off Front Street she passed a frame office building. The downstairs offices were shared by a physician and dentist. She saw a sign pointing to an outside staircase that led to a second floor office: "Indian Bureau, Nathan T. Rouse, Government Agent."

After boarding her horse, Molly carried her valise back to the Shoshone House. She ordered a bath and checked into a room on the back corner of the first floor. The one window looked out toward the tracks and water tower beyond the depot.

Molly closed the curtain and undressed. Her clothes smelled of coal smoke after the long train trip across Wyoming, and she felt gritty from cinders blown into the passenger coach through open windows.

After unbuckling the strap that held the derringer to her thigh, she slipped off her underclothes. Skin as creamy as ivory, the rich curves of her hips led to a flat stomach beneath her full, shapely breasts.

Molly pulled a robe out of her valise and put it on, tying the belt snugly around her waist. Picking up the Fenton file marked "Holcomb," she crossed the room to a wicker rocking chair by the window.

The room was small but comfortably furnished with a brass bed, an oil lamp on the night table, and along the far wall stood an oak washstand with a towel rack. A porcelain basin and pitcher of water were on top. Bathtubs were in rooms at either end of the hall, and while one was being readied, Molly reviewed the papers in the file.

The facts of the case were reported in newspaper clippings from the *Crowheart Journal*, a tri-weekly publication that served most of the county. Through the spring season a number of shootings on Pitchfork range land had been reported to County Sheriff

Wilbur Timmons. Several cowhands had been wounded, and many had quit. The mysterious shootings culminated two weeks ago in the murder of Isaiah Holcomb.

Two investigations—one by Timmons and one by the army—produced no suspects or arrests. Indians from the neighboring Shoshone reservation were generally blamed for the killing, and it was obvious from the newspaper clippings that feelings in Crowheart ran high.

Letters to the *Journal* demanded the removal of the whole tribe. "Ship them to Oklahoma Territory," one correspondent wrote, "and we shall rid ourselves of two afflictions, thieving savages and drunken soldiers."

In an editorial John L. McGrath, editor of the *Journal*, reminded his readers that "the murderer has yet to be apprehended. We must not jump to tragic conclusions. All responsible residents of Crowheart decry the vigilante spirit that is smoldering in some quarters hereabouts."

Molly unfolded the military map supplied by General Holcomb. She found Crowheart on the blue line that was the Wind River, and traced her finger northward to the headquarters of the Pitchfork Ranch. The cattle ranch, twenty-thousand acres in size, covered grasslands north of the river all the way to the timbered foothills of the Owl Mountains. Back in those mountains lay the huge Shoshone reservation. Camp Lincoln, the military outpost housing troopers responsible for patrolling the reservation boundaries and keeping the peace, was located in the foothills along the black line marking the boundary between the ranch and the reservation.

Molly read the obituary of Isaiah Holcomb, and was struck by the differences in the two brothers. Each in his own way had earned fame in the West. As young men they had served in the Civil War with the Twenty-fourth New Jersey. Zachary stayed in the army after

Appomattox while Isaiah came West with a small herd of cattle and an ambitious idea.

In time Zachary came West, too, eager for promotion. The one brother warred against the Indians while the other made peace with them.

Molly's thoughts were interrupted by a knock on the door. "Bath ready, ma'am," came a woman's voice.

Molly put the papers in the file and left the rocking chair. She opened the door to find an Indian woman, who smiled, looking up at Molly's face.

"Bath," she repeated, gesturing for Molly to come with her.

Locking the door, Molly followed the hotel maid to the end of the hall, she caught the beckoning scent of steaming hot water.

The maid was a strong, stout woman who wore her black hair in two braids. Moccasins were on her feet, and she wore a plain cotton dress with an apron.

Three bathrooms were at this end of the hall, and the maid opened the middle one. Just as she turned to point to the tub of steaming water, a man leaped out, brandishing a bayonet.

The maid's terrified scream was cut off when the man slugged her, his fist striking her squarely on the jaw. The force of the blow drove her back to the wall. Her knees buckled and she sank to the floor.

Whirling around, the man thrust the bayonet toward Molly, his eyes flashing. He was unshaven, his sunburned lips scabbed, and his shirt and gray army trousers were caked with dirt and filth. He came slowly toward Molly until the point of the bayonet was under her chin.

"That your bath I was fixing to climb into?" he asked.

"You can have it," Molly said.

He grinned, eyeing her. "Say, you're a real looker, ain't you? Why don't the two of us go in there? We'll lock the door and sink into that hot, soapy water together." With his other hand, he reached out and yanked her robe open. "Say, look at them big—"

"Walk out of here right now," Molly said, "and I won't turn you in. I won't say a word, and you can leave here a free man."

"Hell, I'm free right this minute," he said, "and I aim to enjoy it."

"You're a deserter, aren't you?" Molly asked.

"I've quit the damned army," he said, "and soon as I get cleaned up, I'll catch a night freight out of this stinking state." He leaned closer, his breath quickening as he grasped one of her breasts with his rough, dirty hand. "Now, you come in here with me and we'll have us a good time."

The maid groaned, and the deserter glanced down at her. In that moment the point of the bayonet moved away from Molly's throat. She leaned back, braced herself against the wall, and thrust her knee into his crotch, hard.

Caught off guard with his legs spread, the deserter's eyes rolled back as he let out a shrill, agonized cry. He doubled over, mouth stretched open. A slashing blow to his wrist from Molly's hand sent the long-bladed bayonet clattering to the floor.

Molly quickly moved behind him. She placed her foot on his tailbone and shoved. The deserter stumbled headfirst into the wall. Sprawling to the floor, he drew his knees up and lay there whimpering.

Molly pulled her robe around her and knelt beside the hotel maid. "Are you all right?"

The Indian woman gave her a glassy-eyed nod, and tried to get to her feet.

"Easy now," Molly said, placing a hand under her arm.

"Hey, what's going on down there?"

Molly helped the woman to stand, and turned to see the desk clerk coming down the hall. He approached cautiously.

"We were attacked by this man," Molly said.

The clerk reached the prone figure and said in disgust, "Soldier." He looked first at Molly, then at the maid. "You've been told a dozen times to keep these bathroom doors locked. Drunken soldiers sneak in here—"

"Door . . . locked," the maid said, bowing her head as she spoke.

"Don't lie to me, Indian," the clerk said angrily.

"Look at the bayonet," Molly said.

The clerk turned to her in surprise. He was a slender, balding man with small, dark eyes. "What?"

"Look at the soldier's bayonet," Molly said again. She picked it up and pointed to flecks of white paint on the blade. "Check that bathroom window, and I think you'll find that he used this bayonet to force it open from outside."

The clerk glared at her, then turned and rushed into the steamy bathroom. In a moment he returned, now avoiding Molly's gaze.

"I'll take care of you later," he said in a low voice meant for the maid. Muttering that he would send for the sheriff, he strode down the hall, arms swinging briskly at his sides.

The Indian woman reached out and touched Molly's arm. "Thank you," she whispered.

CHAPTER III

Molly finished her bath and had returned to her room, dressed, and towelled her hair dry when she heard the knock on her door. She had been expecting it.

Opening the door, she found an armed man wearing a badge on his vest. He was in his fifties, she estimated, with deep lines around his eyes and streaks of gray in his hair that was normally covered by the battered hat now in his hand.

"Miss Owens? Miss Molly Owens?"

"You must be Sheriff Timmons," she said.

He blinked. "That's right." After a pause he asked, "I need to make a report on the . . . incident. I couldn't get much out of the Shoshone woman. Mind if I ask you a few questions?"

"Not at all," Molly said. "Come in."

She closed the door behind him and showed him to the wicker rocking chair. He sat down, but did not lean back. Placing his forearms on his knees, he watched her sit on the edge of the bed.

"Exactly what happened?" he asked.

"The hotel maid had drawn my bath," Molly said, "and when she took me down the hall to show me where it was, we were confronted by that man. He punched the maid, and came for me with his bayonet."

"He tried to stab you?"

"He held it at my throat," Molly said, "and tried to force me into the bathroom."

"But you didn't let him," Timmons said.

"That's right," Molly said.

"The desk clerk thought that soldier was drunk and passed out," Timmons said. "I found out different when I hauled him to the jailhouse. You handed that bluecoat a whipping, Miss Owens—pure and simple.

15

He's a big, strong man, too." The lawman regarded her for a long moment. "Just how did you do it?"

Molly shrugged. "I managed to defend myself."

Timmons stared at her, unblinking. "That you did, Miss Owens, that you did. He's the most docile prisoner I've taken in a long while." He asked, "May I ask what your business is in Crowheart?"

"No business at all, sheriff," Molly said. "I'm here to visit my cousin, Nell Holcomb—to visit and pay my respects."

"I see," Timmons said. At the mention of "Holcomb," he lowered his gaze.

Molly asked, "Has anyone been arrested for the murder of Isaiah Holcomb?"

"No," Timmons said through pursed lips.

"Any suspects?" Molly asked.

Timmons exhaled, as though suddenly tired. He stared at the hat in his hands. "Truth is, Miss Owens, I haven't even dug up a single clue. Best I can figure is that someone passing through, rustlers maybe, killed him and rode out." He added, "Maybe Indians did it."

"Tell me about your investigation," Molly said.

He looked at her. "Well, I reckon you have a right to know, being related, and all." He pursed his lips again, remembering. "The body was found in a meadow about five miles east of the ranch house—"

"On Pitchfork land?" Molly interrupted.

Sheriff Timmons nodded. "In a meadow in the forest bordering the Shoshone reservation. Two cowhands had been gathering strays in those timbered foothills, and they were bringing out a bunch when they found the body. They brought the body home, leaving the cattle behind. The ranch foreman, Joe Pardee, sent word to me, but by the time I got to the scene of the killing the cattle had wiped out any tracks the killer might have left. I searched long and hard, but never found a trail to follow."

"How was he murdered?" Molly asked.

"Stabbed," Timmons said. "The cowhands found a trade knife sticking out of his chest."

"Trade knife?" Molly asked.

Timmons nodded. "It's an ordinary, all-purpose knife with a hickory handle and a blade about six, eight inches long. A lot of them have been traded to the Indians over the years. But plenty of whites carry them, too. In fact, a lot of women have one or two around the kitchen."

"So that doesn't point directly to a Shoshone as the killer, does it?" Molly said.

"No," Timmons said. He added, "Unless you don't like Indians."

"Any idea how long Isaiah had been dead when the cowhands found him?" Molly asked.

Timmons cocked an eyebrow. "You're asking all the right questions, Miss Owens. You ever worked in law enforcement?"

Molly smiled and shook her head.

"Near as I can figure," Timmons said in answer to her question, "Isaiah was murdered at about one in the afternoon. He was found a couple hours later."

"Was he robbed?" Molly asked.

"His revolver and Winchester were gone," Timmons said. "He didn't have any money, but he might not have been carrying any."

"Most people here seem to think he was killed by Indians," Molly said. "But why would an Indian leave his knife behind?"

"I don't know the answer to that one."

"Did the army investigate?" Molly asked.

"Colonel Stobaugh looked into it," Timmons said, "but didn't come up with anything. I'm telling you, Miss Owens, there just wasn't a clue to be found."

Molly nodded that she understood. "Did Isaiah Holcomb have enemies?"

"Most folks liked him," Timmons said. "Any man as powerful as he was stepped on some toes over the years, but if you're asking if I know anyone who wanted him dead, the answer is no. He wasn't a hated man."

For a long moment Sheriff Timmons gazed at Molly, then abruptly got to his feet. He put on his hat.

"Well, you ended up asking me more questions than I asked you, but I thank you for your time. I can thank you for Colonel Stobaugh, too. That bluecoat was a deserter from Camp Lincoln, and I know Stobaugh will be mighty glad to get him back."

Molly stood as the lawman moved to the door. He reached for the handle, but stopped in mid-stride and looked back at her.

"The murder of Isaiah Holcomb touched a lot of lives around here, Miss Owens," he said. "It damn near killed his wife. Everyone in Crowheart is upset about it. Folks want me to run down the killer, just like that." He snapped his fingers.

"I've got an election coming up in three weeks," he went on, "and right now I don't stand a chance of being reelected. Never mind the fact that I've worked hard on this investigation. Never mind the fact that I've served this county well for four years. All folks can talk about is why I haven't brought Isaiah's killer in."

He cast a longing look at Molly, as though seeking understanding and sympathy from her, then abruptly said goodbye and turned away.

Molly closed the door after the lawman, realizing that this case had embittered him. He had said things to her, a stranger, that had obviously been gnawing at him for a long time, words deeply felt that he could not speak to anyone he knew.

Molly went to the window and pulled the curtain aside, thinking back over their conversation. Timmons was probably more of a law enforcer than an investigator, and she had an idea that while he had uncovered some clues, he simply hadn't recognized them.

CHAPTER IV

At daybreak Molly took her horse out of the Smythe Livery Barn and rode through Crowheart. She followed Front Street and the railroad tracks past the shops and rooming houses and cafes, all with shades drawn at this early hour.

Molly passed a darkened saloon called The People's Choice, and a board-and-batten building next door. Elaborate gold lettering on the plate glass window read, "*Crowheart Journal*, Ever Faithful to Truth, John L. McGrath, Editor." A sign over the door read, "Job Printing."

On the outskirts of town the road and railroad tracks parted. The rails, now gleaming from the light of the rising sun at Molly's back, followed the course of the Wind River. The road angled through the last of the fenced pasture land that surrounded Crowheart, veering away from the trees marking the river. Ahead lay open range.

Three miles away from town Molly came to a fork in the road. This one had been circled by General Holcomb on the military map. The ranch road cut toward the Owl Mountains on the northern horizon. Molly turned onto this road and followed it only a short distance before she saw cattle bearing the distinctive Pitchfork brand.

The grasslands sloped up toward the timbered foothills at the base of high, snowy peaks. From this distance the Owl Mountains were deep purple, with patches of white at the highest elevations. Those snow fields and glaciers gave birth to all the creeks that flowed into the Wind River, greening pastures and watering stock along the way.

For more than a mile the rutted ranch road followed the course of a tributary to the Wind River. The water in the creek, clear and sparkling as cut diamonds, gurgled and splashed its way downslope over a bed of sand and rounded stones.

After two hours of steady riding Molly drew near the timbered foothills. Shouldered against the high mountains, the hills were covered with ponderosa pines and Douglas firs. She was stirred by the beauty of this land. Not only the majestic sight of it, but the fresh smell of grass, the sounds of the creek and call of birds exhilarated her.

The first white explorers had been led here by a teen-aged Shoshone woman, Sacagawea. In 1812 she had been buried here, having accomplished her mission of returning to her people. Molly wondered if the explorers, Lewis and Clark, had also been struck by the beauty of this land, when her horse topped a grassy hill and she saw the log buildings of a ranch ahead, reminding her that the country was becoming settled and civilized now.

She followed the road downslope toward the buildings. They were dominated by an enormous log barn. In the grass in front of the main house was a sky blue pond, and several geese fled through the high grass as Molly approached.

At the bottom of the slope Molly rode through the ranch gate. Two hand-hewn poles supported a crosspiece overhead. Hanging from that crosspiece was a pitchfork with rusted tines and a long, weathered handle.

The ranch house was an impressive log building overlooking the pond and the wide sweep of grassland beyond. Small windows were on either side of the front door, and a veranda ran the length of the house. Riding closer, Molly saw a swing there and a pair of chairs made from elk antlers.

Fifty yards from the house stood a long, low building that must be the bunk house, Molly thought, and the small cabin nearby was the domain of the second most important figure on any working cattle ranch—the cook.

Molly reined up at the hitching rail at the bottom of the veranda steps. The front door slowly opened, and after a long moment a pair of moccasined feet emerged through the doorway, followed by a set of small wheels.

The white-haired woman who pushed herself onto the veranda was confined to a cane and wicker wheelchair. Her arms as thin as twigs, she grasped the vehicle's large rear wheels with her bony hands and rolled to a stop at the front edge of the veranda.

"Yes?" she said, squinting at Molly.

After introducing herself, Molly pushed her Stetson back on her head and smiled. The wizened old lady stared at her through bright, dark eyes, but made no reply.

"Are you Mrs. Holcomb?" Molly asked. "Mrs. Nell Holcomb?"

"Why, yes," she replied. After a long pause she said, "I don't believe I've made your acquaintance before. Have I?"

"No," Molly said, "but I was told you'd be expecting me."

"You were?" Nell Holcomb said, shocked. "Who on earth told you that?"

Molly glanced around to be certain no one was in earshot, feeling ridiculous as she did so. "General Zachary Holcomb."

"Oh, my!" Nell said, raising a hand to her mouth. "Zachary sent someone, after all. . . ." Her voice trailed off. "Well, you're here, I reckon, come on in, young lady. What'd you say your name was?"

"Molly Owens," she said, dismounting. She tied her horse and climbed the four steps to the veranda, smiling again at Nell Holcomb. The woman was clearly baffled by her presence, and probably a bit frightened.

Molly watched while Nell expertly turned the wheelchair and rolled into the ranch house. Molly followed, closing the door. The room she entered was very large, and possessed a strongly masculine atmosphere.

Glass eyes stared down at her from the heads of elk, deer, and antelope that hung from every wall. A variety of handmade chairs, some covered with cowhide, were grouped around a massive stone fireplace. Over the mantle a Henry rifle hung on wooden pegs.

Nell wheeled herself over the furry hides of grizzlies and brown bears to the blackened hearth of the fireplace, and swung around. She pointed to one of the chairs.

"You're an investigator of some sort?" Nell asked.

"Yes," Molly said, sitting down. "I'm an operative for the Fenton Investigative Agency."

Nell stared at her, seemingly at a loss for words. "If my husband were here, he'd know what to do." She added rather lamely, "But if Isaiah were alive, you wouldn't be here."

"General Holcomb is concerned about you," Molly said.

Nell nodded. "Yes, I know he worries." She ventured a smile. "I'm surprised he didn't send the whole army."

Molly saw a hint of warmth and humor that must have been a stronger part of her personality before her husband's death.

"You can tell Zachary to stop worrying," Nell said. "I'm doing very well under the circumstances." She added, "And tell him the Pitchfork is in good hands with Joe Pardee ramroding the outfit."

"I'll tell him," Molly said. "But in the meantime I'd like to stay here a few days."

Nell met Molly's gaze. "You mean you want to find out for yourself if what I'm saying is true."

"I don't disbelieve you, Mrs. Holcomb," Molly said, "but I want to satisfy myself and General Holcomb that I've done the job I've been hired to do."

Nell looked away. "Well, I suppose Zachary must be satisfied, as you say."

"If we keep my identity a secret," Molly said, "I can conduct a discreet investigation, and no one will be the wiser."

"How can we do that?" Nell asked.

"General Holcomb suggested that we tell people I'm your cousin who's here for a short visit," Molly said. "I can come and go as a sightseer and no one will think it's unusual."

"No, I suppose not," Nell said. She thought a moment, and smiled. "You know, it would be nice to have some female company around here for a change. I suppose you can use the guest bedroom . . . but, oh my, it has to be dusted. That room hasn't been cleaned in months, I'm ashamed to say. I just don't get around like I used to."

"Let me help," Molly said with a wink, "as a good cousin would."

A girlish expression of conspiracy came to Nell's face, and she smiled again at Molly.

Molly smiled, too, not wanting to show her real concern. She was here to conduct a murder investigation, and did not know where the trail would lead.

CHAPTER V

Molly stabled her horse in the big barn where she met the Pitchfork wrangler, Bud Reims. Bud was a lanky man with a game leg. Along with feeding and doctoring animals, his job included shoveling out stalls and repairing corrals.

"Keeps a broken-down cowboy busy," he said with a grin.

Bud admired Molly's gelding as he pulled off the saddle, and went on to say he was glad Nell would have some company.

"I don't believe she has any friends in town," he said, "and now that old Mr. Holcomb's gone, all she does is sit in that house and brood. The doc says she should be up and around instead of sitting in that contraption all the time."

Bud slapped his game leg. "After the horse fell on me last spring, I never thought I'd walk. But soon as I healed up, the doc prodded me out of the bunk and old Mr. Holcomb gave me plenty of chores to do around the place. That's why I'm on my feet today."

Molly walked back to the ranch house. She had heard Bud's voice warm with affection when he'd mentioned "old Mr. Holcomb." Entering the house, she walked down the narrow hall off the front room to her bedroom.

The bedroom was simply furnished with an iron bed, a six-drawer mahogany dresser with a bevel-edged mirror, and a kerosene lamp hanging from a hook on the log wall. The window opened out to a field of flowering lupines behind the house. As Molly looked out there, she saw a granite gravestone.

She changed to a navy blue dress with mother-of-pearl buttons and met Nell in the dining room off the

24

large front room. A door opened into the kitchen. On the other side of it, Nell explained, was a mess hall where Lun Sing fed the cowhands.

Lun Sing was the Chinese cook who brought the noon meal into the dining room. A small man with quick movements, he served a delicious meal of beef and vegetable dishes. He wore a white apron over baggy clothes, sandals on his feet, and his head was shaved, save for a spot in the back where his coal black hair was braided into a queue that hung down to his waist.

After a dessert of canned peaches and fresh cream, Molly saw Nell look out the dining room window. Beyond the pond where half a dozen geese rippled the water was a stretch of grassland spotted with white-flowered beardtongue. A group of horsebackers came through the field toward the ranch buildings.

They were led by a broad-shouldered man wearing a Stetson and riding an iron gray quarterhorse. The cowhands followed him to a pole corral adjoining the horse barn.

"I was sitting right here," Nell said softly, "when they brought him in. Right in this spot . . . waiting supper."

She turned to Molly. "I'll never forget that day. They brought my Isaiah in, slung over the back of his horse. I knew right away he was . . . gone." Her voice trailed off as her eyes closed. "I wanted to die, too."

Molly reached across the table and held her bony hand. Tears dropped from Nell's eyes and followed deep lines down her face.

Moments later a deep, commanding voice came from the kitchen, and Molly heard spurs ringing with heavy footfalls. Nell raised a napkin to her eyes and wiped tears away as the kitchen door opened.

"Bud tells me we got us another pretty lady on the Pitchfork."

Molly turned in her chair and saw that the man who had entered was ruggedly handsome with a squared jaw, pale eyes, and a nose that was crooked at the bridge. A mustache drooped down around his lips.

"Joe," Nell said, her face brightening, "I want you to meet Miss . . . my cousin . . . Miss Molly Owens. She . . . she'll be visiting for a spell."

A terrible liar, Molly thought, hearing the hollow tone in Nell's voice.

"Molly, this is Joe Pardee, my ranch foreman," Nell said.

Pardee came a step closer, holding his tan Stetson in one hand. Molly caught the strong odor of whiskey from him.

"Pleased to meet you, Mr. Pardee," Molly said.

"Call me Joe," he said. "Nell, where have you been keeping this pretty cousin of yours?"

After an uncomfortable silence, Molly realized Nell was at a loss for words.

"I lived back East until recently," Molly said. "When I moved to Denver, I decided I should come to Crowheart and visit my relative."

"Well, now, that's mighty nice," Pardee said. "Now Nell can jaw with someone besides me and Lun Sing. Neither one of us talks good."

"We'll do some visiting," Molly said, "but I'm not one to sit around. I brought my saddle horse. I want to see the sights around here. Nell told me I could have the run of the place."

"Well, sure," Pardee said, his grin fading. "Only right now we're a mite busy, rounding up stock for the Shoshones. Nobody's going to have time to escort you around—"

"I can find my way," Molly said. "And don't worry, I won't bother your riders or your stock."

"Well, all right," Pardee said, turning to Nell. "That's the reason I'm here, Nell. The Shoshone contract is due. Yesterday I ran into Mr. Rouse on the road from town and he said he'd bring the papers by this afternoon."

"I don't know why I have to sign them every month," she said.

"Because you own the Pitchfork, Nell," Pardee said. "We're getting top dollar, and we don't have to pay railroad shipping charges. We just drive them to the reservation, and that's that."

"I know," she said with a tired sigh.

Pardee winked at Molly and turned away. "Feed these hungry men," he called to Lun Sing.

Molly pushed Nell out to the veranda, and after some gentle persuasion she helped her onto the swing. The swing had a wide seat of slats suspended by two chains bolted to a roof beam. Molly sat beside her and started them swinging back and forth.

Nell smiled as she looked out at the peaceful scene in front of the ranch house. She began to reminisce about her life on the Pitchfork and how she had come here a quarter of a century ago.

Nell had grown up in Kansas City and was engaged to marry a railroad man. The engagement lasted several years, and she knew that behind her back people predicted she would become an old maid. Then by chance she met a rancher who had shipped cattle to the stockyards.

"The first time our eyes met," she said, "we knew we'd found each other. We got married in a hurry, and I left home." She looked at Molly. "I may have hurt a man's feelings by breaking the engagement, but as I used to tell Isaiah, I knew a railroader who almost married the wrong woman." A twinkle came into her eyes.

Nell helped her husband run the Pitchfork Ranch. Working side by side they survived winter storms and summer droughts, fighting all the large and small battles of raising cattle and managing men. They never had children, although they practically raised a few runaway boys over the years, runaways who passed through Pitchfork range, worked a few seasons, and moved on. One had stayed. He was Joe Pardee.

"Folks might say we had a hard life here," Nell said, "and I reckon we did. But it was a good one. I believe we both knew that every night when our heads hit the pillows. I'd close my eyes, hear my husband breathing beside me, and think back over the day. Next thing I'd know, morning had come and I'd get up and start the next one."

Seven months ago Nell had slipped on a patch of ice and hurt her hip. The doctor came from Crowheart and told her she had either sprained or cracked her hip. He ordered her into a wheelchair.

"I'm supposed to walk a little every day," Nell said, "but I just don't feel like making the effort any more." She paused as she looked out at the flowers beyond the still pond. "I just want to live out my days here on the Pitchfork, that's all. The best days of my life started here, and I reckon they should end here, too."

"This is a beautiful place," Molly said.

"Heaven on earth," Nell said, rocking gently in the swing. "That's what my Isaiah always said."

Molly asked, "Where was he going that day?"

Nell turned to her. "You mean the day he . . ."

Molly nodded.

"I believe he was riding to Camp Lincoln," she said. "Yes, he was. He left here at noon, saying he had business with Colonel Stobaugh."

"You'd been having trouble with Indians from the reservation?" Molly asked.

"No!" Nell snapped. "Oh, I know some folks in town think Isaiah was killed by Indians, but it isn't true and don't you believe it for a minute. The Shoshone loved him. They remember all those hard winters when he gave them Pitchfork beef."

Nell shook her head. "No, my husband made peace with the Shoshone many years ago, even before I came out here. The whites forget that, or they don't know it. All some folks want is to get rid of the Indians. Isaiah figured we had to live with them. He used to remind folks that the Shoshone were here first."

Nell paused and added grimly, "His murderer will never be found."

"Why do you say that?" Molly asked.

"Because I think he surprised some rustlers," Nell said, "and they killed him and hightailed it out of here."

"Is that what the county sheriff believes?" Molly asked.

"Sheriff Timmons doesn't know what to believe," Nell said. "It's Joe's idea, and I think he's right. We lost several head of cattle in the spring to rustlers, and Joe believes they came back for more. Of course, Isaiah was never one to back down and he probably tried to bring them in. That would be like him."

"Was your husband on his way to Camp Lincoln," Molly asked, "or on his way back the day he was killed?"

"Why . . . I don't know," Nell said. "I never thought to ask anyone."

"Did he tell you why he wanted to talk to Colonel Stobaugh?" Molly asked.

"No," Nell said.

"But he said it was important," Molly said.

"Yes," Nell said. "Isaiah often went to see the commanding officer at Camp Lincoln."

Molly heard a screen door slam and turned to see the cowhands file out of the mess hall. They walked toward their corralled horses with Pardee leading the way, smoking a hand rolled cigarette.

The Pitchfork riders looked like typical ranch hands, Molly thought. High-heeled boots gave them a rocking stride peculiar to men who spent their working days on horseback. They all wore light cotton shirts, dark vests, and Stetsons. Most of them carried sidearms. Several wore knives sheathed on their belts.

Molly considered the commonly held theory that Isaiah Holcomb was murdered by a stranger, possibly a rustler. But that overlooked the fact he had been stabbed in the chest. To Molly, that suggested the killer was known to the victim. Isaiah Holcomb might even have been killed by a friend.

CHAPTER VI

The driver of the one-horse buggy that rolled into the ranch yard later in the afternoon was a pudgy man in a pinstriped suit, white shirt, and tie, and on his head a bowler hat was cocked jauntily to one side. Molly had heard the vehicle coming and stood now at the window as the man reined his horse to a halt at the bottom of the veranda steps.

"Who is it? I heard someone come into the yard."

Molly turned and saw Nell wheel out of the hall that led to the bedrooms. Her face was puffy with sleep.

"A man in a buggy," Molly replied. She moved to the front door and opened it as Nell rolled her wheelchair toward it.

"Mr. Rouse," Nell greeted the driver of the buggy. "Come in. Will you have pie and coffee?"

Molly moved into the doorway behind her and saw a short, round-bellied man coming up the steps. He took off his bowler as he reached the top. Balding, his face had a merry expression with round cheeks and a cherubic mouth.

"Oh, no thank you, Mrs. Holcomb," he said, crossing the veranda. Surprise registered on his face when he saw Molly.

"I'd like you to meet my cousin, Mr. Rouse," Nell said. "She's come for a visit." Glancing over her shoulder, she introduced Molly, and said, "This gentleman is the government agent for the Shoshone reservation, Mr. Nathan Rouse."

"A pleasure to meet you, Miss Owens," Rouse said. "I'm glad to see you have company out here, Mrs. Holcomb, and such lovely, charming company at that."

Molly managed to smile at the gratuitous compliment. "Why, thank you, Mr. Rouse."

After coming into the ranch house, Rouse reached into his breast pocket and brought out a cluster of folded papers.

"I've brought the contracts," he said, "in which the Pitchfork agrees to deliver seventy-five head of cattle to the Shoshone reservation. I need you to sign two copies—one for my files and one for Washington."

After the contracts were signed at a rolltop desk in a corner of the front room, Nathan Rouse made cheerful small talk about the weather, and discreetly inquired how long Molly would stay. Then he clapped the bowler on his head, giving the brim a tug so that it was cocked to one side, and left.

When the door closed, Nell said, "Isaiah never liked that man."

"Any particular reason?" Molly asked.

"Oh, I don't know of any one reason," Nell replied. She paused thoughtfully. "Isaiah used to say there has to be something wrong with a man who's that happy all the time."

Molly grinned. "Nell, I wish I'd had the pleasure of meeting your husband."

On the face of it, the Pitchfork was no different from any other large cattle ranch Molly had seen. The routine here was a common one, well established.

She had risen early enough in the morning to see the cowhands straggle sleepily out of the bunkhouse into the dawn. High-heeled boots scuffing on the plank floor, the men trooped into the mess hall for breakfast.

Lun Sing started a pot of coffee down the long table where the fourteen men sat facing each other, then passed platters heaped with scrambled eggs, bacon, and bread fresh out of the oven. Butter and honey were on the table. The cowhands ate in silence, and then went out to the horse corral beyond the barn.

Bud Reims had herded saddle horses into the corral, and Molly went outside to watch as the cowhands eyed

the stock over a morning cigarette while Joe Pardee
gave out the day's assignments.

When Pardee said, "Let's ride," cigarettes were
squashed under the pointed toes of boots, and men
entered the corral with lariats in hand.

Each man roped the horse of his choice, then
saddled and bridled his mount and swung up. The cow
ponies bucked with morning friskiness while their
riders held on, swearing steadily, until the rodeo was
over.

"Hell of a way to shake down breakfast," Molly
heard one of the cowhands grumble.

While Pardee and the cowhands rode out in their
separate directions to mend fences, clean water holes,
and tend cattle, Molly walked back to the barn. She
went inside and found her buckskin gelding in one of
the stalls.

After saddling the big horse, she led him outside
and swung up. With a wave to Bud who was in the
blacksmith shed, she rode away, heading for the
timbered foothills to the north. According to Nell, this
was the direction Isaiah Holcomb had ridden on the
last day of his life.

Ahead, the foothills that rumpled against the Owl
Mountains were heavily forested by ponderosa pines
and Douglas firs. Molly rode toward them, angling
northeast to follow the route she had plotted on the
military map last night. She and Nell had studied that
map, found the mountain meadow where her husband
had been slain, and marked the most direct route to
Camp Lincoln.

The open grassland, broken by a few ravines, sloped
up toward the trees. As Molly gained elevation, she
looked back at the ranch buildings and the wide sweep
of pasture lands beyond.

Molly wondered if Isaiah Holcomb had known he
would make his fortune here the day he first saw this
country. Chances were that he had known it, Molly
thought, and having come from the smoke, blood, and

screams of Civil War battle, she could easily understand why he called this land "heaven on earth." Grass and water were here for as many cattle as he could raise, and the timberlands provided wood for fuel, logs for buildings and corrals, and posts for fences.

Movement caught Molly's eye as her gaze moved across the wide panorama, and she purposely turned away from it. Perhaps it was only a deer or a stray steer, but if it was a horseman she did not want him to know he'd been seen.

As soon as she reached the cover of the trees, she reined up and tied her horse. Taking a pair of field glasses out of her saddlebags, she walked back to the tree line. She remained concealed as she raised the glasses to her eyes and peered through the boughs of a pine tree. She focused on the ravine where she had detected movement.

In that spot she saw nothing, but as she brought the magnified field of vision upslope, she glimpsed a tan Stetson. It appeared to be moving through the grass of its own accord, bobbing slightly as it came toward the trees.

Molly lowered the glasses. A horse and rider down there were concealed in the ravine.

Cowhand, she thought. *Is he hunting strays, or following me?*

CHAPTER VII

Molly followed a game trail through the pines and stands of thick firs as she angled toward the crest of the ridge. Her progress was slow, as she stopped frequently to listen. She heard nothing but the calls of jays and other birds and an occasional gust of wind whisper through the pine boughs.

Topping the forested crest of the hill she dropped down the far side to the bottom. A dim trail cut through this narrow valley. Molly turned her horse and followed it knowing that she now rode along the boundary of the Pitchfork Ranch and the Shoshone reservation.

Ten or twelve miles from here, due east, was Camp Lincoln. But only a short distance ahead, in a place where this little valley broadened, lay the meadow marked on the military map. The meadow was distinctive because of a strawberry-shaped pond in the middle of it. At the edge of that pond Isaiah Holcomb had met his killer.

While riding for the next three-quarters of an hour Molly carefully watched her back trail. Still she saw nothing, heard nothing. The birds quieted. She could not rid herself of the sensation of being followed or watched.

In the soft ground she saw deer tracks and knew that trailing a shod horse through this valley would be a simple task. She began thinking of ways to use this fact to her advantage, to trick anyone who might be following her. Then she saw a break in the forest ahead, and a patch of still water.

Molly reined up at the edge of the meadow. The pond amid high grass and wildflowers was accurately drawn on the military map. It was a small body of water shaped like a strawberry.

Riding out to water's edge, Molly dismounted. Her horse drank noisily through the bit while she looked around. Surrounded by forest, the marshy ground here was covered with the tracks of deer, elk, and cows.

Molly looked back toward the game trail that had led her here, and devised a plan.

Leaving the horse, she hurried back the way she had come. Reaching the point where the game trail emerged from the forest, she veered off to the side. She made her way through the dense forest, paralleling the trail for twenty yards. She halted.

Molly drew her revolver and knelt down between a pair of towering ponderosas. From here she could watch a stretch of game trail and see her horse at the pond. The gelding was content to stay there, grazing in the lush grass.

The wait was not a long one. In a few minutes Molly heard the clink of a bridle chain and the creak of saddle leather. Looking through needled pine branches, she saw movement. A horsebacker came up the trail, riding slowly.

As the gray horse passed by, Molly edged around one of the ponderosas. She came out on the trail behind the rider just as he reined up. Molly realized he had seen her horse in the meadow ahead.

"Raise your hands, mister," she said, aiming her revolver at him.

Startled, the man half-turned, reaching for his gun. Molly aimed high and squeezed the trigger.

The sound of the gunshot sent the horse prancing, and the rider lost his balance, spilling from the saddle. Cursing, he rolled over, Stetson falling from his head. He was Joe Pardee.

"What the hell are you doing?" he shouted, rising up to his knees.

"That's just what I wanted to ask you," she said. "You've been following me since I left the Pitchfork."

Pardee's eyes widened as he failed to conceal his amazement. Then his face reddened with anger and he got to his feet. "I was following you for your own damn good. A woman shouldn't be riding out here, alone. This is Indian country."

Molly met his angry gaze. If his concern for her safety was legitimate, he'd certainly kept his distance. She remembered that his first reaction a moment ago had been to reach for his gun. She did not lower her Colt .38.

Molly motioned toward the meadow behind him. "That's where the body of Isaiah Holcomb was found, isn't it?"

Pardee stared at her, his expression turning from anger to suspicion. "Just what are you after? Why are you packing a gun?"

"For the same reason you do," Molly said. "Sometimes a person needs one." She repeated her question.

"What if it is?" he replied.

"Nell told me about this place," Molly said. "I wanted to see it for myself."

"Damned foolish," Pardee said. He stooped down and picked up his Stetson.

"Where was the body when you got here that day?" Molly asked.

Pardee did not reply. He put on his hat, turned, and caught his horse. He swung up into the saddle, ignoring the fact that Molly still aimed her revolver at him.

Pardee turned his horse and came toward her. "I don't know what the hell you think you're doing, Miss Owens, but I can guarantee you one thing. Ride this country alone and one day you'll get yourself hurt. You might even disappear." Without warning, he put his spurs to the horse.

Molly leaped aside as the gray quarterhorse charged. Pardee's knees brushed her as he swept past, and she spun away. She'd have been trampled if she hadn't reacted quickly.

Molly watched the foreman gallop away, rounding a bend in the trail. She took a deep breath, and holstered her revolver. Turning, she started down the trail toward the meadow. That was when she saw the Indians.

CHAPTER VIII

Half a dozen Shoshone warriors, mounted on spotted ponies, watched from the trees at the edge of the meadow. Still as statues, the men stared at Molly.

In that instant of discovery Molly realized why she'd felt such a strange sensation ever since she'd come over the forested ridge from the Pitchfork and dropped into this little valley. The sensation had not come from Joe Pardee who had been following her at a comfortable distance, but from these warriors who, Molly sensed, had been at close range all this time.

The men were naked from the waist up, wearing leather headbands that held a variety of feathers. Several carried old rifles, and the others had revolvers and knives stuffed into the belts of their trousers. The trousers appeared to be army cast-offs.

At some unspoken signal, the Shoshone men turned their horses and rode back into the trees. They quickly disappeared into the shadows.

Molly walked along the game trail to the meadow where her horse waited. Strangely, she had not been frightened by the sight of the Indians. They were not menacing—unlike Joe Pardee.

Molly mounted her horse and rode out of the meadow, following a creek that meandered out of the pond. According to the map, the creek flowed past Camp Lincoln eight or ten miles from here.

The bright sun was high in the sky when Molly emerged from the dense forest. The valley flattened out, and pines and firs gave way to a thick growth of willows along the creek and clumps of aspen trees. Their leaves fluttered in a breeze.

In a clearing half a mile ahead Molly caught sight of white canvas tents. Drawing closer, she saw that

Camp Lincoln was a small outpost made up of two rows of fifteen tents, a log building at either end, some sheds, and horse corrals.

She judged the building at the far end to be the officers' quarters. A flag flew there. The nearest log structure, with several black stovepipe chimneys sticking out of the shake roof, must have been the mess hall and day room for enlisted men.

At the camp's perimeter she was met by a uniformed guard who carried a Springfield carbine. A private, he wore a blue coat and gray trousers, and as he stepped forward to present arms and confront Molly, he seemed utterly amazed to see a woman on horseback, alone.

"I'm here to see the post commander," Molly said. When the young soldier only stared at her, she added, "Is Colonel Stobaugh here?"

"Oh, yes ma'am," he replied suddenly. Half turning, he pointed to the building at the far end of the compound. "The ol' man, I mean, Colonel Stobaugh, he should be over there in HQ."

"Thank you," Molly said with a smile. She rode past the young soldier.

Off to her right, several yards beyond the row of tents, she noticed another soldier standing guard over a trio of men digging a new latrine with picks and shovels. Molly saw that they were in chains, and their uniforms bore no insignia.

As Molly rode past, she recognized one of the prisoners. Turning from his work to look at her was the deserter who had tried to assault her in the hallway of the Shoshone House.

The open ground between the two rows of white canvas tents was a parade ground, Molly realized, as she guided her horse toward the flagpole in front of the headquarters building. At sunrise every morning, as in military posts across the country, the soldiers assembled here for reveille, facing the flag.

The tents were empty now. Except for the guard detail, all the soldiers must have been out on patrol.

The door of the log building swung open as Molly approached. A bareheaded officer came out onto the plank porch. Molly saw that he was a colonel. Into the doorway behind him came a lieutenant. He was followed by an enlisted man who was probably the company clerk.

The colonel moved to the edge of the porch. Placing his hands on his hips, he watched Molly ride to the tie rail.

"Colonel Stobaugh?" she asked.

"That's right," he said, looking at her with unconcealed curiosity.

Molly introduced herself and swung down from the saddle. After looping the reins over the tie rail, she came to the porch. The colonel was a handsome, well-groomed man with a distinguished bearing. His uniform was immaculately clean, and his black riding boots were polished to a high shine. Long sideburns came down the sides of his jutting jaw, and his dark brown hair was combed back from his forehead, adding an air of severity to his expression.

"I rode over from the Pitchfork," Molly said.

Stobaugh repeated her name. "I believe I heard about you from Sheriff Timmons. You were assaulted by one of my troopers, weren't you?"

Before Molly could reply, Stobaugh went on, "If you're here to press charges, Miss Owens, I can assure you that the man is being punished in full accordance with military regulations—"

"I'm not here to press charges, colonel," Molly interrupted. "I want some information."

Colonel Stobaugh gave her an icy look. He evidently was not a man accustomed to being interrupted. He asked, "What sort of information?"

"Sheriff Timmons told me the army investigated the murder of Isaiah Holcomb," Molly said. "I'd like to know the results of the investigation."

He studied her. "What is your interest in the case?"

"His widow is my cousin," Molly said. "We both want to know what's being done to apprehend the murderer."

"I see," Stobaugh said. "Well, I can assure you, Miss Owens, that everything in our power is being done—"

"Was he killed by Indians?" she asked.

"Miss Owens, I have no obligation to comment on a military investigation to a civilian," he said.

"I know you don't," Molly said. "But Isaiah Holcomb was an important man in Wyoming. Everyone wants to know what's being done to bring in the killer— everyone from saloon swampers to state senators."

Stobaugh's expression revealed nothing, but he grew silent as he considered the implication of Molly's words. He motioned to the open door behind him. "Come inside, Miss Owens."

Molly stepped up onto the porch, seeing the two men in the doorway quickly duck inside as the colonel turned around.

Stobaugh showed Molly into the outer office of Camp Lincoln's headquarters. Two desks dominated the room, and as Molly passed through the room the lieutenant and the enlisted man, a corporal, busily searched through papers in an oak file cabinet. She sensed that both men looked after her.

Leading Molly into his office, Colonel Stobaugh closed the door. He told her to take the chair in front of his desk, then moved to his own high-backed chair behind it.

On the wall behind him was a map that was similar, but much larger, to the one General Holcomb had given her. It showed the entire Shoshone reservation in a pale yellow shading. As Molly looked up at it, Stobaugh glanced over his shoulder.

"The army in its great wisdom has given me ninety-four troopers to patrol the boundary of the reservation," he said, turning to her. "It's a full-time job, one that most officers and enlisted men learn to hate. My desertion rate is among the highest of all military outposts in the West." He added, "I won't bore you with statistics, Miss Owens, but I want you and Mrs. Holcomb to have some perspective on what I am about to tell you."

Molly watched as a pained expression came to his face. "I took over this command three months ago." He paused. "I might as well tell you this was a punitive assignment. It was handed to me at Fort Robinson after I had engaged my commanding officer in a violent argument. I was offered this assignment or a court-martial. As you may know, the army has a way of offering choices that are not truly choices. So I shipped out here to find myself in command of two captains who had been given similar choices and ninety-four troopers who hate this assignment."

He cast an ironic smile at Molly and went on, "You may be wondering what all this has to do with my investigation into the murder of Mr. Holcomb. Well, I want you and Mrs. Holcomb to know that on the day of his death I had the camp telegrapher wire an urgent message to HQ that we needed a full investigation out here." He paused. "HQ, Miss Owens, is Fort Robinson."

"I see," Molly said. "You did not get much cooperation, I suppose."

Stobaugh nodded. "Lip service, at best. I was ordered to conduct a preliminary investigation myself. If I uncovered evidence that Indians were involved, my request would be considered. Otherwise, I am to stay out of a civilian matter."

"Is that what this is," Molly asked, "a civilian matter?"

"I couldn't find any evidence to the contrary," he said, turning his hands palms up on the desk top. "The Pitchfork cowhands who discovered the body were moving cattle out of the trees. They were shocked, naturally, by their discovery, and all they could think about was taking the body back to the home ranch.

The cattle they left behind milled around, trampling any sign the killer may have left."

Molly nodded that she understood the dilemma. "I'd like to know your own opinion, colonel. Do you think he was murdered by an Indian?"

"I don't know," Stobaugh said. "I honestly don't. I understand the older men of the tribe had great respect for Mr. Holcomb. But this is a new age, and the next generation of warriors has taken over leadership. Young Shoshone men like Eagle-in-Flight and Elk Bull are eager to prove they're worthy of leadership."

Stobaugh turned in his chair and pointed to the map on the wall. "Here's where we are, and up in this basin at the foot of the Owl Mountains is the main Shoshone encampment." He ran his finger in a line to the shaded area of the big map. "I rode in there with Mr. Rouse to act as interpreter and talked to some of the old men as well as a few of the young warriors. I couldn't raise any evidence that a Shoshone had murdered Mr. Holcomb."

He turned back to Molly. "I'm new here, Miss Owens, but I've come to believe that we're sitting on a powder keg. My patrols are regularly finding so-called hunting parties off the reservation, and the young warriors in them are sensitive about being ordered around. We haven't had any trouble yet, but now the whites in Crowheart are agitating to get the whole Shoshone nation shipped out of Wyoming." He paused. "And here I sit with ninety-four troopers to keep the peace."

Before leaving, Molly learned that Colonel Stobaugh had not spoken with Isaiah Holcomb on the day he was murdered, nor had he any idea why the rancher was coming to see him.

On her way back to the Pitchfork Molly mentally reviewed all that she had learned since her arrival in Crowheart, and thought back on her meeting with Stobaugh.

The colonel viewed the murder as one more incident in a larger problem, and worried about how he could keep the peace. But as Molly reflected on the bits and pieces of information she had gathered, she saw another possibility. Someone might be trying to exploit the "powder keg" Stobaugh had described.

First thing tomorrow she would ride to town to interview Nathan Rouse.

CHAPTER IX

In Crowheart the next morning Molly stopped first at the telegraph office in the train depot and wrote a brief report to Horace Fenton in New York City. Written in a simple code that to anyone else would appear to be a pleasant message between friends, Molly handed it to the telegrapher and watched him turn to his key and tap out the words.

Out on the boardwalk that ran the length of Front Street, Molly was hailed by Sheriff Wilbur Timmons. She turned and saw him approach with another man at his side.

"Miss Owens," Timmons said, touching a hand to his hat, "I'd like you to meet John McGrath, editor of our newspaper. I was telling him about the way you handled that deserter, and he said he wanted to meet you. I reckon he wants to do a story on you."

Molly smiled politely at the sheriff, and looked at McGrath. He had a hawklike face, an intense expression that befitted a man who was not afraid to go against public opinion. Molly had realized he'd done that in his editorials following the murder of Isaiah Holcomb. Resisting a groundswell of public outrage took courage, particularly in view of the fact that McGrath depended on local advertisers for most of his income.

"I don't want to be the subject of an article like that, Mr. McGrath," Molly said.

The newspaperman grinned and shook his head. "First, call me Jack. Second, don't let Wilbur scare you off. What I had in mind was to simply mention that you're a visiting relative of Mrs. Holcomb's, and perhaps mention the fact that you'd had an encounter with a deserter from Camp Lincoln."

45

"I must request that you don't write about me," Molly said.

McGrath's grin faded. "Do I detect a note of disapproval toward newspapermen in your answer?"

"Not at all," Molly said. "In fact I'm one of your readers. I thought your editorial on the Shoshone issue was excellent."

The compliment brought a smile to McGrath's face, but he cast a measuring look at her. Commenting that it was a pleasure to have made her acquaintance, he extended his hand.

Molly shook hands with him, and bid the two men good morning. She turned and followed the boardwalk toward the side street that led to Rouse's office. She had recognized a shrewdness in the newspaperman that both interested her and put her on her guard.

Molly crossed Front Street, lifting her skirt as she made her way between a farm wagon and a passing stagecoach. On the next corner she turned and walked down the boardwalk to the frame office building where the sign pointed to an outside staircase. At the bottom she looked up and saw that the door, which swung out, was half open.

As she climbed the stairs she heard an argument raging. Rouse's voice was raised in anger. Molly heard the tear-choked voice of a woman. A moment later came the sound of padding footsteps.

An Indian woman wearing a plain cotton dress rushed out the door and plunged down the steps, nearly colliding with Molly. Her bronze face shone with tears.

Molly spoke to her as she lunged past, but the woman did not pause. At the bottom of the staircase she ran, disappearing around the front of the building. Molly had recognized her. She was the maid at the Shoshone House.

Molly continued up the steps. At the landing she looked into the office and saw Rouse in profile. He was seated at a rolltop desk, face reddened, and when he

caught sight of Molly, his head snapped around as
though ready for another confrontation. But in an
instant his expression changed and he smiled, standing to greet her.

"Miss Owens," he said, "what a delightful surprise.
Come in, please come in."

"I'll come back another time if your prefer," Molly
said. "I can see you've had a problem this morning."

"Problems come with my job, Miss Owens," he said.
"Do come in. Have a seat." He gestured to a Windsor
chair near the desk.

"That woman works at the hotel, doesn't she?" Molly
asked as she came into the small office and sat down.
She saw a pair of large file cabinets along one wall, and
in the far corner of the room was a steel safe on
casters.

"Worked," Rouse said, emphasizing the past tense.
He smiled grandly. "The Shoshone see me as a father
to the whole tribe, and when I can't undo the trouble
they've gotten themselves into, they don't understand
why. That woman was hired at the hotel on my
recommendation. Now that she got herself fired, she
can't understand why I won't simply recommend her
again." He laughed softly as though Molly would
understand the woman's folly.

"What did she do?" Molly asked.

"Oh, I don't know all the details," Rouse said.
"Something about not doing her job properly, leaving
some doors unlocked or something." He added, "Believe me, Miss Owens, she wouldn't have been fired
without a good reason."

"I recognized her because she drew a bath for me
when I first arrived in Crowheart", Molly said. "We
had a little problem with a deserter, and the desk clerk
wrongly accused her of leaving the bathroom door
unlocked."

Rouse's smile faded. "Well, I honestly don't know if
she was fired over that particular matter, or not. As I
say, I feel certain that there was good reason to let her

go." He paused. "You know, Miss Owens, these Indians are wonderful people, but they're simple people. And they don't take to work as we do. They really don't understand working at a job as you and I do. Some days they show up three or four hours late, and can't understand why anyone would be upset about it." He chuckled again.

Rouse gazed at her, and said, "Well, now, how are you enjoying your visit with Mrs. Holcomb? That lady has certainly brightened since your arrival."

"We've talked a great deal, Mr. Rouse—"

"Call me Nathan, please," he said. "May I call you Molly?"

She nodded. "In talking with Nell, I've learned that she knows very little about the circumstances of her husband's death—"

"Why, that's true of all of us," Rouse interrupted. "I only wish Sheriff Timmons would bring in the murderer, and put this terrible matter to rest."

"Do you believe Isaiah Holcomb was killed by Indians?" Molly asked.

Rouse did not answer immediately, but gazed at Molly. "As much as I hate to say it, the evidence points in that direction."

"Do you have any idea who might be guilty?" Molly asked.

"I certainly do not," he said, voice rising.

"I was thinking that you must know the Shoshone as well as anyone," Molly explained, "and that you might have some idea who was guilty."

"If I had any information," Rouse said, "I'd take it to Sheriff Timmons. I want the killer apprehended, believe me."

"I understand that," Molly said, "But it's your opinion I'm seeking. Do you have any particular suspicions about the identity of the murderer?"

With an eyebrow raised, Rouse said, "You certainly ask a lot of questions."

"These are questions that Nell and I have asked ourselves," Molly said.

"Well, now," Rouse said with a smile, "why don't you women leave the investigating to Sheriff Timmons? There's no need to bother yourselves with this sort of thing when you two could be visiting." He paused. "How much longer do you plan to stay?"

Molly returned the man's artificial smile, remembering that he'd asked the same question at the ranch house. "A few days," she replied.

Molly returned to the Smythe Livery and got her horse. Although she was dissatisfied with the interview and the progress of her investigation, she was getting a sense of the place, a feel for the texture of life here.

Every region in the West that Molly had been sent to work as an operative for the Fenton Investigative Agency was different. The differences were more than terrain or individual men and women she came to know. Each region possessed qualities of the familiar and the new in the flow of people's lives, a blend and clash of personalities that taken as a whole made a unique human fabric. As an outsider, and as a trained investigator, Molly found that she could not only see this fabric but examine it more closely than an insider.

Molly had recognized almost immediately that the fabric of life here had been slashed by the murder of Isaiah Holcomb. Now as she rode out of Crowheart she thought about the people she'd met, and considered what any one of them had to gain by the murder of the most prominent ranchman in this part of Wyoming.

But suddenly she was distracted by the sight of a lone figure walking in the road ahead. As Molly rode closer, she recognized the Indian woman she'd seen running out of Nathan Rouse's office, who was trudging down the road now, carrying a bundle.

"Hello," Molly said, drawing rein beside her. The woman did not look around until Molly said, "Remember me?"

The Indian woman looked up, her large brown eyes blinking against the bright sky.

"We met in the Shoshone House," Molly said.

The woman nodded. "Today . . . no want you see me."

Molly smiled that she understood, and dismounted. As Molly came around her horse, the woman drew back a step, holding the bundle to her chest. The bundle was a gray wool blanket gathered at three corners. Molly had seen other blankets like it covering bunks in the tents at Camp Lincoln.

"What you want?" the Indian woman asked.

Molly saw not fear but distrust in her eyes, and then heard a whimper. Seeing the woman clutch the bundle, Molly suddenly understood the reason for her protectiveness.

"You have a baby, don't you?" Molly asked. "May I see?"

The woman stared at Molly for a long moment, then looked down and pulled aside a corner of the blanket. Molly came closer and saw the bright eyes of a six- or seven-month-old infant. Lips moving, the baby was obviously ready for the next meal.

Molly said, "The Indian agent told me you'd lost your job at the hotel," Molly said. "Was it because of the soldier who broke into the bathroom?"

The woman eyed Molly, then nodded once.

"I'll go back there with you," Molly said. "I think I can clear this up so you can get your job back."

"No!" the woman said, shaking her head vigorously.

"I know you were treated unfairly, but—"

"No!" she exclaimed. "I no go back!"

Molly looked at her questioningly, surprised by this strong reaction.

"Rouse say I have job," she said.

"At the hotel?" Molly asked.

The woman nodded.

"I don't understand," Molly said. "Rouse said you could have your job back?"

She nodded emphatically.

"But you don't want it?" Molly asked.

"Yes, I like . . . work," she said.

Confused, Molly asked, "Then why don't you go back?"

"No!" she said. "I want no more baby!"

"What?" Molly asked.

The Indian woman reached out with her free hand and touched Molly's breast, then her own. "You woman, I woman. Rouse, he say I lay with him. Get job back."

"Oh, I understand," Molly said. Now she knew why the Indian agent had yelled at this woman. Molly grasped her hand. "Where are you going?"

The woman pointed toward the Owl Mountains, but a forlorn look came into her eyes. "No man there for me. Have no one."

Molly squeezed her hand. "I want you to come with me."

CHAPTER X

Her name was Morning Star and by birth she was half Shoshone and half Crow. The Crow Indians were ancestral enemies of the Shoshone. Battles no longer raged between the two tribes, but even now Morning Star's dual heritage prevented her from being fully accepted by either tribe. She had spent time living with both, but in recent years she'd lived among the whites, having learned enough English to work at a variety of jobs in Crowheart.

Nell had heard of Morning Star and was delighted to learn that she wanted to work on the Pitchfork. Since Molly's arrival, Nell had become concerned about the ranch house's appearance and had been frustrated by her inability to keep the place spotlessly clean. Morning Star was the answer to a prayer.

At first the Indian woman said she and her baby would sleep in the horse barn. Nell would not hear of it. She insisted they move into the bedroom next to Molly's.

While Molly helped ready the room, she questioned Morning Star about the Shoshone reservation and again heard the names of two young warriors, Eagle-in-Flight and Elk Bull. Morning Star confirmed what Molly had heard from Colonel Stobaugh. The two warriors had recently assumed power, and now were ready to prove their worthiness to lead the tribe.

Molly also learned the Owl Mountains were considered to be sacred ground by the Shoshones. According to the story behind the Indians' belief, Morning Star said, the Crow and Shoshone chiefs journeyed alone deep into those mountains. They met in a secret place and engaged in mortal combat. The battle was long and bloody as one strong warrior wounded the other.

But at sundown the bloodied Shoshone chieftain stood over his foe, and in a final act of triumph he cut the heart out of the fallen enemy's breast.

"Crowheart," Morning Star said when she concluded the story, telling Molly where the name had originated.

Now only on certain occasions, with permission of a medicine man, did Shoshone tribesmen venture into the sacred mountains. No white man had ever traveled into those remote valleys and canyons.

After Nell introduced Morning Star to Lun Sing and told her that her first job would be to help him clean up the kitchen after the cowhands were fed this evening, Molly took her outside and showed her around the ranch. In the horse barn she met Bud who welcomed her to the Pitchfork.

Among Morning Star's other chores, she was to take over the laundry from Lun Sing. Molly showed her the lean-to adjoining the back of the ranch house. Opening the door that squealed on rusty hinges, Molly pointed out the wash tubs, scrub boards, and cakes of lye soap stored there.

On the Pitchfork Morning Star would earn sixty cents a day, the same salary she'd been paid at the Shoshone House. But here that salary included three meals a day and a room, and more important, she was wanted and needed.

Tears showed in her brown eyes as she thanked Molly. In Crowheart she'd slept winter and summer in a shack on the bank of the Wind River, and with other Indians had eaten fish she'd caught and small animals she had trapped; these were cooked by throwing them directly into the flames of an evening campfire. Now in the privacy of the lean-to Morning Star opened her dress to show welts where a clerk at the hotel had caned her.

"And they named that hotel after your people," Molly said, shaking her head. But the irony was lost on Morning Star. She embraced Molly and hugged her.

That evening Molly went into the horse barn where half a dozen cowhands were gathered around a stall discussing the possible merits of a newborn colt. Bud Reims held a lantern, and as Molly joined the group she heard him describe the birth before dawn this morning.

"That little mare was having some trouble," he said, "and when I heard her, I came and eased things along a mite."

Looking between the shoulders of two cowhands, Molly saw a patch of white in hay piled at the back of the stall. The colt's mother stood nearby, eyeing the soft-talking humans.

"Evening, Miss Owens," Bud said.

The cowhands turned, reaching for their Stetsons to greet her. Molly had seen these men in the mess hall or walking across the yard, but had not been introduced.

"Miss Owens, have you met Charlie Sands?" Bud said. "And this here's Sam Olson, and this tall drink of water is Butch Burns."

Molly shook hands with each of the cowhands as she was introduced to them, all young men who had spent a good deal of their lives in the saddle. The remaining three were Hank Leeds, George Fowler, and Phil Strenge.

"Pleased to meet you, gentlemen," Molly said after she had shaken the last rope-callused hand.

"First time anyone ever called me that," Charlie Sands said, chuckling.

With no trace of a smile, Butch said, "I'm not a bit surprised to hear that, Charlie."

The others laughed as Charlie elbowed him in the ribs.

"Miss Owens," Hank Leeds began. He paused before launching into his question. "Any truth to the rumor that you've come here to take over the Pitchfork?"

Molly was surprised by the question, but when the cowhands fell silent and stared at her, she realized this had been a source of much discussion.

"No, there isn't," Molly said. "I'm here for a visit, that's all."

"Well, you being blood relative and all, we just thought . . ." Hank's voice trailed off.

Phil Strenge said, "And the way you handle that big gelding of yours, we figured you're the one to run this outfit."

Molly smiled, shaking her head. "I'm flattered that you men believe I could do the job. But Nell is boss, along with Joe Pardee."

After an uncomfortable moment, Bud said, "Truth is, Miss Owens, these hands stayed on out of loyalty to Mrs. Holcomb, not for any love of Pardee."

"I see," Molly said. "He does have an unfriendly way about him, doesn't he?"

"Lately, he's needed a bigger hat," George Fowler said.

"What's he getting a swelled head over?" Molly asked.

"Pardee claims he'll be taking over the Pitchfork afore long," Butch said.

"Then he must know something Nell doesn't," Molly said. "She has no plans to leave. This is her home."

Molly went on to ask about the murder of Isaiah Holcomb, but if any of these cowhands held private theories about the identity of the killer, none spoke up. They seemed satisfied that either an Indian or a rustler had murdered the rancher.

They were worried about Indians. Hunting parties had been sighted on Pitchfork range, and some had made threatening gestures at men working cattle. Shots had been fired from ambush, and several long-time ranch hands had quit for fear of being gunned down. Replacements hired by Pardee were inexperienced and disliked by the men who had worked many seasons for Isaiah Holcomb.

In the next two days Molly toured the ranch on horseback, spending noontime and long evenings with Nell. Nell had become unofficial grandmother to

Morning Star's baby boy and spent much of her time caring for him, even leaving her wheelchair to pick the infant up or put him down to bed. Talking about the baby, Nell smiled and a glint of happiness shone in her eyes.

Thundering hoofbeats and shouts brought Molly and Nell out of the ranch house after the noon meal the next day. From the veranda they saw three Pitchfork cowhands gallop through the gate to the bunkhouse. One man rode slumped over his horse's neck, obviously hurt.

Molly recognized two of the riders—Butch and Hank. She did not know the injured man by name.

While Hank helped the man into the bunkhouse, Butch spurred his quarterhorse to the veranda. "Indians hit us!" he called out. "Came out of nowhere and started shooting!" He reined up. "We lit out, and Pete got hit in the back!"

"You were on Pitchfork range?" Nell asked, rolling her wheelchair to the front edge of the veranda.

Butch nodded emphatically. "Out in the south pasture."

Nell thought a moment. "Get a fresh horse, Butch. It's too dangerous to ride through the foothills to Camp Lincoln. Ride to Crowheart and send a message by wire to Colonel Stobaugh. Tell him what happened, and tell him we need help."

Butch nodded and turned his lathered horse.

"Come back with the doc," Nell called after him.

Butch waved that he heard, and rode to the horse barn where Bud stood in the doorway, hands on his hips.

Two hours later Joe Pardee rushed into the ranch house, his boots sounding loudly on the plank floor. He'd received word of the shooting and had come straight back after going to the south pasture.

"We found slaughtered cattle," he said grimly. "Four triple wintered steers, Mrs. Holcomb—prime stock. Shoshones butchered them."

"No," Nell whispered.

"Afraid so, ma'am," Pardee said. "We found plenty of Indian sign—tracks of unshod horses and travois marks leading back to the reservation."

Nell shook her head, not in disbelief but in sadness.

"I'm gonna need more men," Pardee said, "eight or ten riders, men who are handy with guns." When Nell did not reply immediately, he added, "Mrs. Holcomb, if we don't protect Pitchfork herds, we'll be picked clean."

Nell nodded, looking up at him from her wheelchair. "Yes, go ahead, Joe. Put out the word that we're hiring."

Molly saw him nod, turn, and stride out of the room. He had never once looked at her.

CHAPTER XI

Events moved swiftly during the next forty-eight hours. An outcry for action that came from the citizens of Crowheart was answered by Colonel Stobaugh. He personally led a detachment of troopers with two field cannons onto the reservation. Reaching the basin in the shadow of the Owl Mountains, he bivouacked within sight of the main Shoshone encampment, aimed his cannons at the Indians, and conducted a search of all the lodges while Rouse questioned tribesmen in an effort to learn who took part in the raiding party.

News of this action by the army came to Molly from Jack McGrath when the newspaperman rode to the ranch. He arrived in the evening to interview the wounded cowhand. After talking to the man in the bunkhouse, McGrath came into the ranch house. Molly greeted him and took him into the dining room.

Over coffee served by Lun Sing, the newspaperman told Molly that Stobaugh and Rouse had left the reservation empty-handed but convinced their point had been made. Stobaugh had made it known that any Shoshone "hunting parties" found off the reservation would now be disarmed and possibly imprisoned.

"Will the warriors take that threat seriously?" Molly asked.

"Who knows," Jack replied with a shrug. "The Indians have a different way of looking at things than we do. If those warriors have decided it is time for a fight, they won't listen to anyone outside their tribe." He added, "They have a strong sense of honor."

"But why are they stirred up?" Molly asked.

"Answer that question," he said, "and you'll have the key to the whole problem. Rouse has a simple answer. He claims the warriors that are now in power are itching for a way to prove themselves and won't be stopped until blood has been shed. That's why most folks in town are saying the whole tribe ought to be shipped out of Wyoming."

"You don't agree with that, do you?" Molly said.

Jack grinned. "Nope." He raised the cup to his lips and drank. "The way I see it is that we all have to live here together, and we have to figure out ways to do it peacefully, red man and white."

"Nell told me her husband used to say the same thing," Molly said.

"Isaiah respected the Indians," Jack said, "and they knew it."

"Then the theory that he was murdered by an Indian doesn't make sense, does it?" Molly said.

"Not to my way of thinking," Jack said.

"Do you think he was killed by a rustler or an outlaw passing through?" Molly asked.

Jack shrugged again, eyeing Molly. "It's possible."

"But you don't think so," she said.

"No, I don't," he replied.

"What is your theory?" Molly asked.

He smiled. "You sound like a journalist, Miss Owens, with all your probing questions." He asked pointedly, "Are you?"

Molly shook her head. "No, I'm not. I'm just interested in your ideas. This murder needs to be cleared up."

"I agree," Jack said. "Do you plan to do that?"

Now Molly smiled, realizing both of them were playing a cat-and-mouse game, with neither willing to reveal all that he knew.

"I think someone has to try," she said. "That's why I'm interested in your theory."

"I don't have a theory about the identity of the killer," Jack said. "But my journalist's nose tells me there is more to this murder than most folks see. I think Isaiah may have been killed by someone around here, someone who's still around here."

"Someone known to Isaiah Holcomb," Molly suggested.

Jack nodded slowly while regarding her.

"What about the killer's motive?" Molly asked.

He grinned. "Now you sound like a lawman." He paused. "I don't have a good theory about the killer's motive. Holcomb was well liked in these parts. I can't think of a reason for someone to want him dead. Maybe the killer's mind is twisted, and he didn't need a reason."

"I've thought of that," Molly said, "but it doesn't explain why the killer tried to make it look like the work of an Indian."

"What's your theory?" Jack asked.

"I don't have one," Molly said, "but I intend to keep asking questions."

"That may not be wise," he said.

"Why?"

"Because the killer may be here among us," he said. "If you get too close, he'll come after you."

Molly watched as Pardee brought more men to the Pitchfork. Within three days of the wounding of the cowhand, he'd hired ten men, all of whom arrived heavily armed.

These men were not cowhands, Molly soon realized. At least they were not men who worked cattle and performed ranch chores as a chosen profession. They were gunmen, and they showed no interest in cleaning water holes or doctoring cattle or doing any of the other jobs that came with ranch work.

After observing these men for a time, Molly suspected many were a step ahead of the law. Where Pardee had found so many hardcases, and so quickly, was a mystery.

The raid on Pitchfork cattle further convinced many residents of Crowheart that Isaiah Holcomb had been murdered by Shoshone warriors. Demands to move

the tribe out of Wyoming were renewed. Even Nell
wavered in her defense of the tribe.

"It's a new generation, like Joe says," she told Molly
one evening after supper. "These young Indians just
don't have the same respect their fathers did. They
don't remember how it was. All they want to do is
make trouble."

"I'd like to find out for myself," Molly said.

"Well, I reckon we can take Joe's word for it," she
said.

"I plan to ride into the reservation," Molly said.

Nell's head snapped around as she looked at Molly in
surprise. "What?"

"I want to see the Shoshone encampment first-
hand," Molly said, "so I'll have a better idea what this
tribe is like."

"It's too dangerous, Molly, much too dangerous,"
Nell said. "You can't just ride in there like a sightseer.
Not nowadays. No telling what those Indians will do."
She added, "Besides, if an army patrol catches you,
they'll slap you in irons. It's the law."

"Then I'll have to be careful," Molly said.

Nell shook her head vigorously. "No, Molly. You
don't know—"

Molly raised a hand and smiled at her. "I'm going."

"This is the scariest, craziest thing I ever did hear,"
Nell said. She stared at Molly for a long moment, the
lines in her face deepening with worry. "Even if you
did manage to find the encampment, you wouldn't be
able to talk to the Shoshone. They're wild Indians,
Molly. They know a few cuss words, and that's about
all."

"I'll ask Morning Star to take me in," Molly said.
She added, "That is, if you can manage the baby for a
day or two."

"Why, sure I can," Nell replied with a trace of
indignation in her voice. She exhaled. "You're determined to go, aren't you?"

Molly nodded.

"What brought on this wild notion, anyway?" Nell asked.

"I have a feeling everyone is overlooking the obvious," Molly said. "I'm not sure what that is, but I'll have a better chance to see it if I can talk to the Shoshones myself. I think I can find out more from them than a bunch of troopers carrying guns and making threats."

"Maybe you're right about that," Nell said. "The army is always heavy-handed. That's what my Isaiah used to say." Nell shook her head again. "But Molly, those Indians are stirred up like a nest of hornets. A blonde scalp might look real good to one of them."

CHAPTER XII

An hour before dawn Molly and Morning Star quietly saddled and bridled her buckskin gelding and a Pitchfork mare. They rode out of the horse barn without awakening the snoring Bud Reims, and left the ranch buildings in night silence.

The moon was down and the sky lighted only by stars. They picked their way across the pasture that led to the timbered foothills, using the same trails Molly had taken the day she'd ridden to Camp Lincoln. This time she would travel straight north into the hills, and Morning Star would lead the way onto the reservation.

In pitch darkness Molly and Morning Star topped the forested ridge overlooking the ranch buildings. Looking back through a break in the trees Molly saw a yellow glow of lamplight in the window of Lun Sing's cabin.

The day dawned quickly as the black sky thinned to pale light. Molly and Morning Star were able to move faster through the trees as they crossed the game trail in the small valley and started up the forested slope of the next hill. From here on Molly followed Morning Star's lead.

The horses labored through pine forests and dense stands of thick trunked fir trees. Over one hill after another, Morning Star avoided well-traveled trails, and she remained watchful through the early part of the day.

At a spring deep in the hills, they stopped to rest and water the horses. Morning Star turned in the saddle and touched a finger to her lips. She pointed to the tracks of unshod horses. Molly nodded. While they had seen no other signs of Shoshones, Molly understood her caution. It would be to their advantage to approach the main village unseen. From a distance they could observe the Indians and try to determined their mood.

The sun had passed its zenith in the sky when Molly saw through the trees ahead to open ground. The great basin Stobaugh had pointed out on his map stretched across to the steep slopes on the Owl Mountains, a stretch of nearly flat land that was rich with grass and wildflowers, and now Molly saw a thick growth of brush where a stream wound through this heartland of the Shoshones.

Morning Star held to the trees, turning east. Slowly, she led the way along the edge of the basin. Presently the terrain lifted. They rode up a forested slope that dropped sharply on the other side.

Molly stood in the stirrups, trying to see ahead, then she ducked down as her gelding brushed past a pine. The horse tossed his head, and now Molly caught the smell of wood smoke in the air. A moment later she heard the sounds of barking dogs and the excited voices of children at play.

Morning Star halted, and Molly reined up behind her. They dismounted and tied the horses, moving toward the crest of the rise on foot.

Molly quickly understood the wisdom of Morning Star's approach to the Shoshone encampment. This rise gave a commanding view of the basin.

Morning Star dropped to her knees and crawled ahead. Molly followed. Shrieks of children grew louder, and she saw a haze of smoke in the air. Morning Star crawled under the boughs of a pine tree, inching ahead. She stopped, motioning for Molly to move up beside her.

Molly used her elbows and knees to crawl under the tree, and then she lay on pine needles beside the Indian woman. The sight in the grassy meadow below brought a gasp of amazement.

The whole Shoshone village stretched out before them. More than two hundred lodges were bunched along the meandering creek. Molly looked at the women working down there, and then her eye was caught by the herds of spotted ponies where the children played.

Their play was work, too, she soon realized. A child would suddenly dash away from his friends to retrieve a pony that had wandered away from a herd and was heading for the trees.

Molly backed out from under the pine and went to her horse. She returned with her field glasses. For the next two hours she and Morning Star watched the Shoshone camp.

All but cradled infants were busy. White–haired women tended the fires where meat was being cooked on spits or stewed in large iron pots that were trade items from the whites. Molly saw hides stretched out, held tight by pegs driven into the ground. Women and young girls scraped the deer and elk hides to remove fat, the first step in the process of tanning to make a soft leather that would adorn one of them or a family member.

Morning Star stretched out her arm and pointed to the trees on the far side of the village. A hunting party emerged from the pines and rode across the meadow toward the lodges.

Molly raised the field glasses to her eyes and brought the riders into focus. Eleven Shoshone men were in the hunting party, and several carried deer carcasses slung over their horses. As they drew near the village, children whooped and several ran through the high grass to meet the returning hunters.

Molly passed the field glasses to Morning Star. She looked briefly, then lowered them and pointed to the big, square shouldered man in the lead.

"Eagle-in-Flight," Morning Star said. "Elk Bull behind him."

Molly took the glasses and looked at the two men as they rode to the lodges. From this distance she could not get a clear look at the face of Eagle-in-Flight, but she saw that he was taller than the others and heavily muscled through his chest. He wore buckskin trousers. In his right hand he carried a rare prize among Indians—a lever-action repeating rifle.

Elk Bull, Molly saw, was a squat, powerful-looking man. He wore a black felt hat, round at the crown with a flat brim. In the crook of one arm he carried an old single shot rifle.

"When should we go in?" Molly asked, watching the hunters ride into the encampment. Women and children excitedly gathered around the men as they dismounted and lifted the carcasses of deer from their horses.

"Soon," Morning Star said, glancing at the sun sinking into the western sky. "They eat, we go."

At sundown Molly and Morning Star left their place of concealment under the pine tree and went to their horses. Morning Star led the way as they backtracked through the forest. A quarter of a mile away, Morning Star turned her mare and swung into the open basin.

"They see us now," she said.

Molly understood. By riding into the village from the open basin, the Shoshones would have plenty of warning and would see that the two women were alone.

They rode through the high grass, angling out into the basin for half a mile. Looking ahead, Molly saw a haze of smoke, and presently the lodges in the meadow below the timbered rise came into view.

Almost immediately she heard a warning shout, and then saw running figures and a flurry of activity in the encampment.

Moments later half a dozen mounted warriors carrying rifles, revolvers, and war clubs came galloping toward them on their ponies. Molly saw Morning Star

halt, and reined up beside her. When the charging
warriors drew closer, Morning Star shouted at them.

The Shoshone men swept past, circling their ponies
to come back. They waved their weapons at Molly as
they milled about. All the while Morning Star spoke
loudly to the men.

"Come," she said to Molly, and rode through the
group of warriors.

Molly followed her to the encampment, and most of
the warriors rode with them. One pulled close and
reached out to touch Molly's skin. Molly smiled at him,
but saw no friendliness in his face.

Children ran out from the lodges to meet them,
pointing and giggling at Molly. They dashed around
the horses until they were shooed away by the warriors. Then they ran ahead to the middle of the
encampment.

In open ground there, around the coals and blackened logs of a recent bonfire, Eagle-in-Flight waited
with Elk Bull. Standing around the edge were women
and several old men.

Molly and Morning Star were escorted into this
opening encircled by lodges. They dismounted, and
their horses were taken away by a pair of young
warriors. Molly stayed with Morning Star as she
approached Eagle-in-Flight, and now she saw his face.

He was a handsome man, copper-skinned, with a
wide nose and dark eyes and a broad chin. In the crook
of one arm he carried the repeating rifle Molly had
seen through the field glasses. While Morning Star
spoke to him, he shifted the Winchester and held it
across his waist.

Lettering on the blued frame of the rifle caught
Molly's 'eye. She stepped forward to Morning Star's
side and read the engraved words: Isaiah Holcomb.

CHAPTER XIII

The moment of discovery in an investigation nearly always brought a surge of triumph that was at once exciting and satisfying to Molly.

But not this time. She stared dumbly at the Winchester in the hands of Eagle-in-Flight, knowing that she had just made the discovery that Colonel Stobaugh and his troopers had failed to make. And she knew, too, that the fate of this proud warrior, and perhaps the whole Shoshone tribe, was now in her hands.

"He say come."

Molly looked at Morning Star, scarcely aware that the woman had spoken to her. Molly nodded, and turned to see Eagle-in-Flight move away. The crowd of Shoshone men, women and children parted as he walked toward one of the conical lodges that ringed this meeting ground.

Molly walked with Morning Star behind the muscular Indian, and saw him duck into the tepee. Built of lodgepole pine logs covered with animal hides, the entrance was a small opening at the base. Decorative drawings of armed men pursuing animals covered the lower part of the lodge, and over them was a large red circle—the sun.

The mixed smells of leather and smoke greeted Molly as she entered the lodge behind Morning Star. Her booted foot sank into something soft and when she knelt beside the Indian woman she realized the floor was covered by a bear hide.

Eagle-in-Flight sat facing them, crosslegged. Molly sat down on the furry hide beside Morning Star.

"I tell him you bring strong medicine," Morning Star said, "and you want to be friend of the Shoshone."

"Does he understand any English?" Molly asked.

"Maybe some words," Morning Star replied. "Most cuss words."

Molly thought a moment while Eagle-in-Flight stared at them. She wondered how she could ask her questions without angering him.

"Tell him that I come as a friend of Isaiah Holcomb," Molly said. While Morning Star made the translation into Shoshone, Molly thought ahead, carefully watching the man's face.

Eagle-in-Flight's reply was translated by Morning Star. "I was friend of Holcomb. My people in big sorrow now. Big hunger."

"Hunger?" Molly asked Morning Star. "What does he mean?"

Morning Star shrugged and spoke to him again. "He say Shoshone hunters kill deer and elk. Have great hunger. No Holcomb, no beef."

"Does he mean Isaiah Holcomb was giving them extra cattle?" Molly asked. "More than the government allotment?"

Morning Star translated the question, and then gave Eagle-in-Flight's reply. "He say same thing. Holcomb dead. Shoshone have great hunger."

"Tell him I want to find the killer of Isaiah Holcomb," Molly said.

Again came Eagle-in-Flight's reply: "Shoshone know killer."

"Who?" Molly asked, her pulse quickening.

"White man," Eagle-in-Flight said. He pointed to his eyes. "Shoshone know."

Molly stared at Morning Star as she translated. "Ask him the killer's name," Molly said.

This time Eagle-in-Flight made no reply.

"Tell him if I find the killer of Isaiah Holcomb," Molly said, "the Shoshone will have no hunger."

Morning Star translated, but still Eagle-in-Flight sat impassively. Presently he stood, moved past them, and ducked out of the lodge. The meeting was over.

"Why won't he tell me?" Molly asked.

Morning Star shrugged. "White man's business not for Shoshones." She got to her feet and moved to the flap of the lodge. "We must go."

"Was he telling the truth about knowing who the killer is?" Molly asked.

Morning Star spoke over her shoulder as she went out. "I think yes."

Outside the tepee Molly saw Eagle-in-Flight and Elk Bull engaged in a confrontation. Speaking in hushed but strong voices, the two men stood facing one another while several Shoshone warriors looked on.

Morning Star whispered to Molly, "Eagle-in-Flight say bring our horses so we may go. Elk Bull say no. Elk Bull no trust you."

The brief power struggle ended when Eagle-in-Flight gave a terse order to a pair of warriors standing nearby. The men obeyed without hesitation, leaving the knot of warriors. Elk Bull turned away, glared at Molly, and left.

When their horses were returned, Molly and Morning Star rode out of the village under the watchful eyes of the Shoshones. Crossing the creek, they struck out across the basin. A short distance away, Molly looked over her shoulder. She saw three warriors following. One was Elk Bull.

The warriors held back a distance of a hundred yards, following the two women all the way across the basin. After entering the timbered foothills, Molly lost sight of the Shoshones, but when they reached the spring deep in the forest Morning Star touched a finger to her lips and then Molly heard horses coming down the slope they had just descended. The Indians were following, but still kept their distance.

They never again caught sight of the warriors. Breaking out of the trees that evening, Molly saw the lamplit windows of the Pitchfork Ranch. Crossing the pasture between the timbered foothills and the ranch buildings, Molly looked back several times. If the warriors were there, they did not venture out into the open.

Over a late supper Molly described the Shoshone encampment to Nell. She related her talk with Eagle-in-Flight, but left out the fact that she had seen the young chieftain carrying Isaiah's Winchester.

"Eagle-in-Flight told me that your husband was murdered by a white man," Molly said.

"Who's he claiming did it?" Nell asked.

"Either he doesn't know," Molly said, "or he didn't trust me enough to tell me."

Nell shook her head. "There was a time when I'd have believed most anything a Shoshone said. But now I don't know. Troublemakers are leading the tribe, seems like."

"The Indians are hungry, Nell," Molly said.

Nell looked at her in surprise. "Hungry? What do you mean?"

"Eagle-in-Flight said that ever since Isaiah died, the Shoshone have been hungry," Molly said.

"No," Nell said, "that can't be true. We're selling the same number of steers to the government that we always have."

"Did Isaiah ever give extra cattle to the tribe?" Molly asked.

"No," Nell said slowly. "I'm sure he didn't. No need to. Between Pitchfork beef and the elk and deer the Shoshone kill on the reservation, the tribe has always been well fed."

"Then I wonder why Eagle-in-Flight says his people are hungry?" Molly wondered aloud.

"Trying to make trouble, probably," Nell said. "I do believe he's a crazy Indian, and he's trying to stir that tribe to war." She added sheepishly, "Nathan Rouse thinks so, too."

"He was here?" Molly asked.

Nell nodded, looking downward.

"You told him where I'd gone?" Molly asked.

"I didn't exactly tell him," Nell said, casting a glance at Molly, "but he sort of figured it out. I guess I let too much slip when he started asking about Morning Star." She added quickly, "But I didn't tell who you are—who you really are. Gosh, I'm sorry, Molly."

Seeing genuine regret in the old woman's lined face, Molly reached out and grasped her hand. "No harm done."

"Mr. Rouse somehow heard that Morning Star was working here," Nell went on, "and came to tell me that with the Indian trouble we're having now, she should leave."

Molly's jaw clenched. This was evidently his revenge to the woman who had refused his advances.

"Well, when I let it slip that Morning Star had taken you onto the reservation," Nell said, "that little smile left his face and he got real mad. He said no whites had any business being on the reservation, and that you'd probably get yourself killed because those Indians are at war."

"They didn't seem to me to be a tribe at war," Molly said.

"Well, maybe you're right," Nell said. "I keep remembering that my Isaiah never did like Mr. Rouse." She added, "And I don't know why Morning Star can't work here if she wants to. I need her." She added, "And that baby gives me a lot of joy." Molly smiled and squeezed Nell's hand. A widow faced with many new situations and decisions, she was proving herself to be a woman who stood up for her beliefs.

Molly thought about Nathan Rouse, and wondered why he claimed the Shoshone were at war, led by a "crazy Indian." If anyone was trying to stir up people, she thought, Nathan Rouse seemed to be doing the job. Why? Tomorrow she decided to look for the answer.

CHAPTER XIV

Molly rode for Crowheart in the morning after telling Nell that her business would probably keep her in town overnight. Shortly after ten in the morning Molly reached the outskirts of town, passed a noisy school yard, and followed Front Street to the train depot.

Dismounting, she tied her horse at the rail and entered the high-ceilinged depot. Evidently no trains were due for the room was empty. Behind a screened window across the room a uniformed ticket agent read a newspaper, and through an open door in the office next to him Molly saw the telegrapher sitting back with his feet up on his desk.

Molly crossed the room and went into the telegraph office. "Is the wire clear? I'd like to send a message to New York City."

The telegrapher was a scarecrow of a man with a green eyeshade on his head. Caught by surprise, he swung his feet down and quickly shoved a sheet of paper and pencil across his desk to her.

"Yes, ma'am," he said, looking at her.

Molly was aware that his gaze lingered on her while she bent down and wrote out a simply coded message, informing Horace Fenton that she was well and her investigation was progressing. She addressed it to "H.F. Jones" at a post office box in New York.

Molly handed the penciled message to the telegrapher and watched him turn to his key and tap it out. So engrossed was she that she was unaware someone had moved close behind her until she was startled by a man's voice.

"Good morning, Miss Owens."

Turning quickly, Molly looked into the hawklike face of Jack McGrath.

"I'd like a word with you," he said. "In private."

Molly met his piercing gaze while the telegraph key tapped steadily. She nodded, seeing an intense and perhaps unfriendly expression in his face.

After paying for the telegraphed message, she left the depot with the newspaperman. They walked to the next block where the *Crowheart Journal* was housed in a frame building adjacent to the People's Choice Saloon. Shown inside, Molly saw an old Washington Hand Press, racks holding trays of type, and a floor littered with crumpled sheets of newsprint and a variety of handbills.

"Excuse the mess," McGrath said, closing the door behind her. "My apprentice won't be in until tomorrow. Come this way."

Molly followed him to the back of the press room where he opened the door to his private office and living quarters. The room was little more than a cubicle containing a desk, a cot, and a coal cookstove. McGrath yanked a swivel chair out from the desk and turned it around for her.

"Sit here, Miss Owens," he said. "I'd just made a pot of coffee when I looked out the window and saw you ride into town. Will you have a cup?"

"Yes," Molly said, sitting down. She noticed that this small room was no cleaner than the press room, and in greater disarray. Blankets were rumpled on the cot. A thick layer of dust covered unused parts of his desk top, and the windowsill was littered with dead moths.

The coffee Molly saw in the chipped porcelain cup McGrath handed her had an oily substance skimming the top. Wondering if it was printer's ink, she raised the cup to her lips. The brew smelled good, but was too hot to taste, and she decided that was just as well as she watched the newspaperman scowl after swallowing.

"I know who you are," he said, setting the cup down amid the clutter on his desk, "and why you're here."

Molly was not surprised. From the expression on his face she had sensed that he knew.

"I've been thinking about you," he said, "about Timmons' description of the way you handled that army deserter, and about the questions you asked me."

He paused. "I have a friend in Denver, a journalist who owes me a favor, and I asked him to do some checking. As a Fenton operative, Miss Owens, you're well known in both the Denver City Marshal's office and the office of the United States Marshal. I'm surprised you didn't come up here under an assumed name."

"Next time I will," Molly said with a smile.

Jack studied her. "You are a cool one, like Timmons said."

"Does he know my identity?" Molly asked.

Jack shook his head. "No one around here knows but me." He asked, "Did Mrs. Holcomb bring you in to find her husband's murderer?"

"Nell did not hire me," Molly said.

"Then who did?" he asked. "You are here to investigate the murder of Isaiah Holcomb, aren't you?" With the question came his piercing gaze.

"You must have learned enough about me," Molly said, "to know that I won't discuss the case."

"Touché, Miss Owens, touché." He paused. "But I wish you had told me who you are. We might be able to help one another."

"I work alone," Molly said.

"Let me put it this way," he said. "I believe I can help you."

"In what way?" Molly asked.

"By sharing information," Jack said.

"If you have any information," Molly said, "I'd like to hear it."

He nodded. "And I'd like to hear yours."

"No deal," Molly said. She glanced around the office. "You have your line of work, and I have mine."

"Printing the news is my line of work," he said, "and your identity is big news around here. If you don't want to cooperate with me, I'll have to run the story as a way to put pressure on the killer—"

Molly set the coffee cup down and stood. "Until you said that, I was starting to like you." She turned and moved to the door.

"Miss Owens—"

Molly walked out of the office and strode across the littered floor of the press room with Jack McGrath coming behind her. He caught up at the front door.

"Miss Owens, you must understand—"

She turned to face him. "No, Mr. McGrath, you must understand that I'm here to do my job no matter what happens. I will not be threatened, and I will not be blackmailed."

Molly turned to the door, opened it, and stepped out onto the boardwalk. She walked away, leaving McGrath with a bewildered look on his face.

Molly crossed Front Street and followed the boardwalk down to the cross street that led to the Indian Bureau office. She paused at the corner, gathering her thoughts. If McGrath revealed her identity in the next issue of the *Crowheart Journal*, or perhaps sooner if he spoke to Sheriff Timmons, she would have to work fast.

Turning the corner, she walked along the street, looking up at the second floor windows of the frame building where Rouse had his office. On the east side the shades were drawn.

Molly passed in front of the building and quietly climbed the stairs. Seeing that the door was closed and locked with a heavy padlock, she breathed easier. She had thought Rouse would still be at Camp Lincoln, but had no way of knowing for certain.

Molly climbed the steps to the landing, and glanced back. The side street was empty, and no one was in sight. She reached into her handbag and brought out a small leather case. Inside was a set of lock probes.

Molly examined the keyhole in the padlock, then selected a probe from the case. Inserting it into the keyhole, she applied upward pressure while withdrawing the probe. The padlock popped open.

Molly removed it and opened the door. Quickly stepping into the office, she closed the door behind her.

The room was hot from the morning sun and had a musty smell. Molly scanned the furnishings, looking at the big rolltop desk, file cabinets along the opposite wall, a bookcase, and a safe in the corner. Framed maps hung on the walls.

Molly went to the desk and pulled the chair out. Sitting down, she put her handbag and the padlock on the floor and tried to open the rolltop. It was locked.

She bent down and looked at the small keyhole, then reached into her handbag and brought out a ring of master skeleton keys. The second to the smallest one fit in the keyhole, and with a single turn released the lock. Molly raised the rolltop.

The pigeonholes and various compartments were filled with recent correspondence and the usual assortment of office supplies, from pens and ink bottles to stationery.

Molly glanced through the papers and pulled letters out of opened envelopes. After scanning the contents, she put each piece back in its place. Most were routine communications and acknowledgements from the Indian Bureau in Washington. One phrase in a letter caught Molly's eye before she went on to another: "Your suggestion regarding transfer of the Shoshone tribe to Oklahoma Territory is now under consideration by the director. . . ."

In the desk drawers Molly found more official letters, along with records and a bottle of rye whiskey. One drawer contained receipts and lists of supplies sent to the reservation over the past three months. Molly examined these closely enough to determine that all the recorded numbers were consistent for that period of time.

After locking the desk, she approached the file cabinets. The drawers were not locked, and she quickly discovered voluminous records of the same type she'd found in the desk. She closed the drawers and went to the safe in the far corner of the room.

She had immediately recognized the safe as one commonly purchased by the government. She had seen the same type in the United States Marshal's office in Denver. They were heavy, fireproof vaults, but uncomplicated.

Kneeling in front of this one, she spun the knob three full turns to the right, then one more while she heard the first set of tumblers fall into place. From there it was a relatively simple matter of turning the knob two turns to the left, listening for the combination that operated six tumblers in succession.

After a final turn to the right, Molly grasped the handle. She turned it. The safe door swung open on oiled hinges.

Molly had no idea what she would find in this safe, but of all the valuables she might have guessed were here, the treasure she found amazed her. Reaching in, she lifted out one of the heavy rocks and held it to the light.

Her first impression had been accurate. This piece of granite, the size of a grapefruit, had a yellow cast to it. Turning it, she saw ore imbedded in quartz, ore that looked pure to her eye. It was gold.

A creak of wood and the light scuff of a boot on the steps outside swung her attention to the door. Molly had time only to put the ore sample on the floor, pull up her riding skirt, and draw her derringer. The office door slowly opened.

CHAPTER XV

"Don't shoot," Jack McGrath said, raising his ink-stained hands as he stepped into the Indian agent's office.

Molly lowered the derringer. "Seems like you've been following me ever since I rode into town."

"You have to admire my taste, don't you?" McGrath said with a grin.

"What are you doing here?"

"I could ask the same question of you," Jack said. He closed the door and crossed the room to where she knelt in front of the safe. "I saw where you were headed after you stomped out of my office. I knew Rouse was gone, and the more I thought about it, the more I thought I'd better have a look."

"Well, your nose for news will get you another story," Molly said.

His gaze went from the ore sample at her feet to the open safe. "What is the story?"

"You tell me," Molly said.

"Look Miss Owens," he said, exasperated, "can't we call a truce? I admit I was out of line. I'm not going to print a story that will reveal your identity, and I won't tell anyone. That's a promise." He added, "All I want to do is get at the truth."

"So do I," Molly said. She met his gaze, and their eyes held for a long moment. "Can we talk off the record now?"

Jack nodded. He held out his hand to shake.

"All right," Molly said, shaking hands with him. She gestured to the ore sample with her derringer. "This is high grade gold ore. The question is, where did Nathan Rouse get it? Is there mining activity around here?"

Jack shook his head as he looked at the chunk of granite at Molly's feet. "No, there isn't. Never has been in this part of Wyoming." He thought a moment. "Maybe Rouse won it in a poker game from someone passing through town."

"His safe is half full of ore samples," Molly said. "Too much for him to lug up here after a night of poker."

Jack murmured agreement. "Makes a man think."

"About what?" Molly asked.

Jack looked at her, his eyes probing. "Where Nathan Rouse could have discovered gold."

Together they went through the contents of the safe, examining the other ore samples and half a dozen reports from an assayer in Laramie. These cryptic reports proved that the samples were as rich as Molly had guessed. The ore ran several hundred ounces to the ton.

After replacing all the ore samples and returning the papers to the safe, Molly closed the steel door and spun the dial. She had not found the one item she needed most—a map. Without one she had no hope of ever locating the granite outcropping where the samples had come from.

Molly crossed the office to the door, opened it a crack, and checked the street for passersby. Seeing no one, she stepped outside and let Jack out of the office. She shut the door and locked it, following the newspaperman down the staircase. At the boardwalk he turned and faced her.

"Where will your investigation go from here?" he asked.

Molly looked at him, but did not reply.

"Still don't trust me, do you?" he asked.

"I told you I work alone, Mr. McGrath," Molly replied.

"Can't we at least be on a first name basis?" he said.

Molly grinned. "All right, Jack. Call me Molly." She paused. "I can tell you this much. I'm going to check into Nathan Rouse."

Jack said, "There is nothing strange about a man being secretive about a gold discovery. If I found a rich outcropping, I wouldn't be talking about it, either. At least not until I'd filed a claim."

"That's just what I mean to look into," Molly said. "I'll telegraph an inquiry to the office of public records in Cheyenne. If Rouse has not filed a claim for a mining property, I'd say that's suspicious."

"Well, yes," Jack said thoughtfully. "But I don't understand what bearing this has on your investigation into Holcomb's murder."

"It may not have any bearing," Molly said, "but if Rouse has one secret, he may have others."

They walked back to Front Street and rounded the corner, heading for the *Journal* building and the depot. The street was crowded with wagon and horse traffic, and Jack took Molly's arm as they threaded their way through it to the opposite boardwalk.

Molly felt his firm grasp. He did not let go after they cleared the traffic, but guided her into the doorway of his building. After a trio of women passed by on the boardwalk, Jack leaned close to her.

"I've never met a woman like you, Molly," he said, "but now that I have, I don't want to be away from you." He paused. "I know this sounds crazy, but from the time I saw you right here on this boardwalk, I've been head over heels in love with you."

Molly said, "Love is a big word, Jack."

"Around Crowheart I'm known as a confirmed bachelor," he said, "and that word doesn't come easily to me."

Molly looked into his eyes. She had never seen vulnerability there before. He was a man who talked fast and hard, ever faithful to the truth, but now his voice was thin and unsure.

"I'm staying at the Shoshone House," Molly said, touching the back of his hand with her fingertips. "I'll be waiting for you this evening." She pulled away and left the *Journal* doorway, walking on to the depot.

After sending off her second telegraphed message of the morning, Molly ate at a nearby cafe and then checked into the Shoshone House. If the desk clerk recognized her or remembered her name, he gave no sign of it. He perfunctorily showed her to a room halfway down the hall of the first floor.

The window of the room looked out on the railroad tracks beyond the depot to a stack of creosoted railroad ties and the dripping water tower. Standing at the window, she heard the mournful wail of a train whistle in the distance.

Molly watched as the train pulled in a few minutes later. The steam engine halted at the water tower. From this angle Molly could not see the departing passengers, but she did catch a glimpse of soldiers climbing down from a coach behind the coal car. Then she saw a pair of army officers on horseback. They rode toward the soldiers. One was Colonel Stobaugh.

Molly hurriedly left the hotel to catch him, and soon realized she need not have worried about missing the colonel. The moment Stobaugh saw her, he turned his horse away from a captain who was taking command of the two squads of troopers lining up beside the passenger coach.

Colonel Stobaugh met her a dozen yards away from the train, and dismounted. "What's this I hear about you traveling onto the reservation?"

"Since you haven't heard it from me, colonel," Molly said, "I'd call that a rumor."

He glared at her. "You can make light of it, Miss Owens, but I promise you one thing. If I ever catch you crossing into Shoshone lands, I'll haul you in and lock you up. I don't play favorites—even to a woman."

"I've never asked for special treatment," Molly said. "All I want are answers to a few simple questions."

"Such as?" he said.

"Why are those Indians hungry for meat?" Molly said.

"Who the hell told you that?" Stobaugh demanded.

Molly smiled. "If I told you, you'd want to jail me."

"It's a damned lie, Miss Owens," Stobaugh said, his voice rising. "If you think I'm taking cattle away from the Shoshone—"

"I don't," Molly said. "I'm just wondering why those Indians say they're hungry."

Stobaugh's face reddened as he seemed too angry to speak.

"I have another question," Molly said. "Has gold been discovered on the reservation?"

He sputtered and swore again. "Where do you come up with these harebrained notions? Damned if you aren't trouble behind a pretty face. Hell no, there isn't any gold on the reservation, and don't you start any rumors about it. I've got enough trouble securing the reservation boundary without a new problem."

"I'm not one to start rumors," Molly said. "This is between you and me. Thank you for answering my questions."

Stobaugh stared at her, mystified.

The detachment of troopers was rapidly drawing a crowd of townspeople. Stobaugh saw them gathering, and swung up into his McClellan saddle and turned his horse. As he rode to join his men, shouted questions came from the men of Crowheart. They demanded to know what was being done about "the Indian problem."

"You gentlemen can see for yourselves," Stobaugh said, holding a tight rein on his horse that pranced in front of the growing crowd. "We're bringing in more troops to secure the reservation boundary. More patrols will be—"

"But what're you doing about finding Isaiah Holcomb's killer?" shouted a man wearing a brown suit and bowler hat.

"We conducted a thorough investigation," Colonel Stobaugh replied, "and found no evidence Shoshones were in the area at the time—"

"Hell, we all know Isaiah was stabbed in the heart by a damned injun," another townsman shouted. "Now they're attacking the Pitchfork. Can't you put a stop to it?"

"The army is doing everything—" Stobaugh began.

"Every Shoshone oughta be run out of Wyoming!" shouted a man wearing a straw hat and farmer's overalls.

"Afore they attack Crowheart!" yelled another man.

"Now, listen here," Stobaugh said, raising his voice. "This town will not be attacked by Indians. We are securing the reservation, and we'll put a stop to this trouble."

"If you don't," a man yelled, "we will!"

"Somebody oughta shoot a few injuns!"

Stobaugh yelled back, "You men listen to me! I'll keep the peace on the reservation. Any man who comes looking for trouble will find more than he can handle." He turned his horse and rode away, joining the troopers who had now mounted their horses and were waiting in formation beside an empty stock car.

Molly watched as the soldiers rode out of town to the shouts and jeers of many townspeople. Some troopers looked back from time to time, but Colonel Stobaugh did not.

After nightfall Molly crossed the darkened hotel room and answered the knock on her door. Easing the door open, she let Jack in. She closed the door and went to him, stepping into his embrace as he found her in the darkness.

She wore a long satin nightgown and when she pressed her body against Jack, she heard him moan with desire. She felt his hands run down her back to the full and firm curve of her buttocks.

"Molly," he whispered. "Molly."

CHAPTER XVI

The reply to Molly's telegraphed inquiry to the state capital arrived late the next day: No mining claims had been registered in the Crowheart region, and no claims in the state were listed under the name of Nathan Rouse.

Molly had left the depot and was halfway across Front Street when she heard her name called. Turning, she saw Jack McGrath step out of the *Journal* building onto the boardwalk. He waved.

Molly turned back and met him on the boardwalk. He wore an ink-splotched apron, and his sleeves were rolled up for work.

"Your answer come from Cheyenne?" he asked.

Molly nodded, and summarized the contents of the telegraphed message.

"Makes you wonder what Rouse is up to, doesn't it?" Jack said.

"I intend to find out," Molly said. She saw warmth in his gaze as he regarded her.

"I know I already told you this," he said, "but last night was the greatest night of my life."

Molly smiled.

"I want to reach out and grab you right here in public," Jack said, grinning.

"But we have work to do, don't we?" Molly asked.

"Sure," Jack replied. "Work. Everyone wants to know about the Indian trouble, and I've got type to set." He added, "Now, I want to help you with your investigation—"

"Jack," Molly interrupted, "I work alone."

"That's what you keep telling me," Jack said. "But after last night things are different. Aren't they?"

"Some things are," Molly said. "But not that one."

"When can I see you again?" he asked.

"Soon," Molly said.

Jack nodded, not taking his eyes from her. "I'm going to help out in this investigation of yours, whether you like it or not."

"I know you mean well, Jack," Molly said, "but don't muddy the water."

"Don't worry," he said. "I won't do anything to compromise your investigation—or your identity. That's a promise." He added with a smile, "But you'd better keep in touch with me in case I come up with some evidence."

"I will," Molly said.

Molly crossed the street to a cafe where she ate, and then went to the Smythe Livery Barn for her horse. As she approached, a short, plump man wearing a bowler emerged from the door. He was Nathan Rouse.

"Saw your horse in here when I got back from Camp Lincoln," he said.

"So you've been waiting for me?" Molly asked.

"That's right," he said. "I had a long talk with Colonel Stobaugh about you. He's convinced you entered the Shoshone reservation. Is that true?"

"Something tells me that no matter how I answer that," Molly said, "I'm in trouble."

"This is not a joking matter," Rouse said. "Are you aware that I have the same powers of arrest as a United States marshal?"

"Congratulations," Molly said.

His expression darkened. "Just because you're a relative of Mrs. Holcomb's doesn't mean I won't treat you the same as any other citizen. Now, answer my question. Did you trespass on reservation land?"

"Mr. Rouse," Molly said, "I don't expect you to treat me differently from any other citizen. And like any other citizen, my travels are my own business."

"Then you won't admit that you trespassed on Shoshone land?" he asked.

Molly met his gaze, and stared him down.

"In that case," he said, reaching out to grasp her arm above the elbow, "I'll have to place you under arrest while I conduct an investigation."

"Let go of me, Mr. Rouse," Molly said.

His cherubic mouth curved into a small smile. "I'm taking you to a cell in Sheriff Timmons' jail. You'll be held there until a U.S. marshal can be sent to escort you to Cheyenne. You'll be arraigned in federal court." His grip on her arm tightened.

"I told you to let go of me, Mr. Rouse," Molly said, bringing her other hand across her body.

"Now, just what does a pretty lady like you aim to do," he asked, "resist arrest?" He started to twist her arm behind her back.

Molly reacted quickly. Her hand shot out, striking Rouse in the throat.

Gasping as his eyes bulged, Rouse turned her loose and grabbed his throat with both hands. He struggled for breath and began choking.

"I don't like being manhandled," Molly said. "Now, what were you saying about arresting me on some trumped-up charge?"

Rouse sucked in a deep breath and exhaled. Pulling his dusty coat aside, he reached to his belt and drew out a revolver. He stepped back and took aim.

"You'll see if this is a trumped-up charge," he said. "Now move!"

Horse and wagon traffic stopped on Front Street and onlookers gathered as Molly was marched at gunpoint to the jailhouse. Inside, Sheriff Timmons looked on in amazement while Rouse loudly preferred charges against her. He charged Molly with trespassing on reservation land and assaulting a federal officer.

Timmons reluctantly took Molly's handbag away from her. While Rouse watched, he led her down a corridor to a single cell at the rear of the building.

Rouse glared triumphantly while the sheriff locked her inside, and then the Indian agent turned and strode away.

"Sheriff, do one thing for me," Molly said.

"What?" he asked.

"Tell Jack McGrath about this," she said. "Tell him I need a lawyer."

Timmons nodded. "I have to stay here until my night deputy comes on duty. He should be here in half an hour. I'll stop by the *Journal* on my way home."

Absurd, Molly thought as she watched the sheriff walk to the end of the corridor and close the door. *This whole thing is absurd.* Timmons evidently had the same reaction, because he forgot to have her searched.

Molly knew the two-shot derringer strapped to her thigh was her ticket out if she had to use it. But that would put her on the run, and she would probably have to return to Denver and turn the case over to another operative.

Better to wait this out, she decided, as she looked around the small cell. She sat on the blanket-covered mattress spread over the bunk, and leaned back against the wall.

Time dragged by, with Molly looking at her time-piece every few minutes. More than an hour passed when the corridor door opened. Molly went to the front of the cell and saw a deputy coming with a tray of food.

"Tell Sheriff Timmons I want to see him," she said.

The deputy was a scrawny young man whose attempt to grow a mustache had left a pale shadow on his upper lip. He stared at Molly, obviously intrigued to see a woman in the cell, and shoved the tray through a slot in the bars.

"What's it worth to you?" he asked.

"Just tell him," Molly said, meeting his cocky gaze. She took the tray of food from him.

"How about if I search you first?" he asked. "You look like you oughta be searched."

"All right," Molly said. "If you think you're man enough, come in here and try it."

"I'm man enough," he said, clenching his jaw. "You look like you oughta be taught a lesson, a good one."

"I'm waiting," Molly said. "In the meantime go get the sheriff for me. Please."

"I'm man enough to have you begging for more," the deputy said. He turned abruptly and walked away.

Hearing the door slam, Molly slapped her hands together. *Where's McGrath?*

Darkness seeped into the cell and Timmons did not come. Neither did the deputy. Molly did not eat the food on the tray—vegetables, a biscuit, and a slice of beef covered with congealed grease in a dark gravy. She drank the water from a tin cup beside the tray, but even it had a foul taste.

Molly lay back on the cot and closed her eyes, thinking she would not sleep. But the next thing she heard was a key rattling in the cell door.

Realizing she had dozed off, she sat up and peered into the faint light coming from a lamp at the far end of the corridor.

"I told you I was gonna learn you a lesson, pretty lady. Now I'm gonna do it."

The cell door squealed on its hinges. Molly saw the shadowy figure of the deputy move toward her.

"Stay away from me," Molly said.

"Don't do no screaming, now. You're gonna like this."

Molly caught the foul scent of his body odor. She drew back. Her foot touched the tray of food on the floor. Quickly bending down, she picked it up and threw it.

The tray hit the deputy and bounced off, clattering to the floor. He swore.

"You hadn't oughta done that."

In the near darkness Molly saw him wipe gravy and vegetables from his face and shirt front. Then he took off his shirt. Molly stood to meet him.

"Get back on that cot."

Molly assumed a defensive stance, resting her weight on the balls of her feet. She heard the deputy breathing as he approached. When he was two paces away, her right foot lashed out.

In the dim light her aim was not true. The toe of her lace-up shoe hit his inner thigh and slid up to his crotch. The deputy yelped in surprise and pain, and cursed as he drew back a fist and swung wildly.

Molly ducked, and felt his fist graze the top of her head. Staying low, she clenched her right hand and drove it into his abdomen.

The blow brought a groan from the deputy, and he backed away, cursing in a strained voice. "Whatsa matter with you, kicking and hitting me? All I want is a little fun."

Molly advanced another step, drew her foot back, and this time her kick did not miss. The point of her shoe banged into his scrotum, doubling him over. A downward blow from the side of her hand struck the back of his neck, and the deputy crumpled to the floor of the cell.

Molly moved to his side, reached down and grasped his limp arm at the wrist, and shoved it up between his shoulder blades. The deputy moaned, then cried out.

"You ready to teach me that lesson now?" Molly asked, planting her knee in the small of his back.

He moaned in pain.

"You said this was going to be fun," Molly said. "Is this fun? Come on, tell me you're having a good time."

In a muffled voice he said, "Damn you to hell."

"Doesn't sound like you're having fun," Molly said. "I'll leave you here. Maybe you can find a way to entertain yourself."

She let go of his wrist and stood up. The deputy moaned again, but made no effort to stand. On her way out of the cell Molly took his keys and pulled the barred door shut.

Following the narrow corridor to the doorway, Molly edged into the sheriff's office. It was illuminated by a lamp on Timmons' desk.

She was surprised to see by the eight-day clock on the wall that the time was 3:10 in the morning. After locating her handbag in a bottom desk drawer, Molly left the jailhouse through the front door.

The starlit street was empty, the town quiet. She followed the boardwalk toward the *Crowheart Journal* building, walking silently and glancing around to be sure she was not being watched. She did not know if Timmons had another night deputy, one who made rounds. Probably not, she decided as she drew near McGrath's building. A second deputy would not be needed in a town this small and this peaceful.

The *Journal* building was dark, as Molly expected, but she was surprised to find the front door unlocked and standing slightly ajar. She stepped inside.

"Jack?"

Staring into silent darkness, Molly saw the vague shape of the big hand press, stacks of paper, and several large containers of printers ink.

"Jack?" Molly said again, louder.

She moved ahead and slowly made her way through the cluttered press room to the back office. As she came to it, she reached out and felt for the door. Her hand touched nothing but air. The door was open.

"Jack?"

When no reply came, Molly reached into her handbag and groped for a box of matches. Finding it, she took a match out and struck it.

She blinked against the bright light that sputtered in her fingers. Stepping into the room, she held the match in front of her and looked around.

Just as the surging flame reached her fingertips Molly's eye was caught by a still figure on the floor. The sight brought a gasp, and in the next instant the flame singed her fingertips.

The match fell into darkness at her feet, but not before she had seen Jack McGrath. He lay on the floor looking up at her through lifeless eyes. A dark handled knife stuck out of his chest, buried to the hilt.

CHAPTER XVII

Sheriff Wilbur Timmons arrived at the *Crowheart Journal* building carrying a lantern. By its pale light she saw a severe expression on his unshaved face.

"You have some explaining to do," he said.

"So does your night deputy," Molly said. After staring at him for a long moment, she said, "Did he tell you that I let him out of the cell so he could get you?"

"He said you busted out," Timmons said.

"If I did," Molly said, "would I be waiting here for you?"

Timmons paused. "We'd better talk about that later. You claim there's a body around here?"

"Inside," Molly said. She turned and entered the building.

Molly led the sheriff through the press room. Their shadows danced crazily in front of them. She halted at the door to the back office and Timmons moved past her. Seeing the still figure sprawled on the floor, he swore in a voice thick with emotion. He knelt down beside the body.

Molly heard the man sob, and she moved into the room and put her hand on his shoulder. He braced his head with his free hand, and the lantern shook in his other hand. Molly spoke soothingly to him. She had cried her tears out.

Timmons took a deep breath, and stood. "I hate this damned job." He cleared his throat, and turned to her. "But I'll run down this killer if it's the last thing I ever do."

"Is that knife like the one that was used to kill Isaiah Holcomb?" Molly asked.

Timmons extended the lantern and took a second look at the handle of the weapon. "It's a trade knife, all right." He swung his gaze back to Molly. "Just what do you know about this?"

"I found him just as you see him," Molly said. "I came to ask Jack why he hadn't answered my call for help. You gave him my message, didn't you?"

"I did," Timmons said.

"Then you might have been one of the last people to see him alive," Molly said.

Timmons acknowledged the point with a nod, and then searched the room. Molly watched as he stooped down and picked up an object.

"What is it?" she asked.

He held up a long, delicate feather.

"Eagle," Timmons said, looking at it by lantern light. "The Shoshones like eagle feathers."

"So you think an Indian did this?" Molly asked.

Timmons turned his gaze to her. "I'd like to know what you think, Miss Owens."

Something in his tone of voice put Molly on her guard, and she did not reply immediately.

"Miss Owens, you know a whole lot more than you're telling me, don't you?"

"I have my theories, sheriff," she replied, "but I'm not withholding any evidence from you."

"After you were jailed yesterday," Timmons said, "I looked through your handbag. Thought it felt heavy. A Colt .38, master skeleton keys, and a set of lock probes add weight to a lady's bag, don't they?"

"Why wait until now to tell me?" Molly asked.

"I didn't think it through until now," he said. "But I'm remembering how you handled that deserter in the hotel. You aren't Nell Holcomb's cousin at all, are you?"

Molly shook her head, no longer seeing any need to keep up the pretense with him. "I'm an operative for the Fenton Investigative Agency."

"A Fenton detective, huh," Timmons said, nodding. "Nell hire you to look into Mr. Holcomb's death?"

"No, I wasn't hired by her," Molly said.

"Then who did?" Timmons asked.

"I'm not at liberty to say," Molly said.

"You'd damn well better talk to me, Miss Owens," he said. "I want to hear everything you know about this case."

"I don't know much," Molly said. "All I can tell you is that I don't think Isaiah Holcomb was murdered by rustlers any more than Jack McGrath was."

"All right," Timmons conceded, "my theory about rustlers is out of the picture. But an Indian could have killed both men." He held up the feather. "Plenty of people are going to be ready to believe that."

"I don't," Molly said.

"Do you have evidence that points to someone?" he asked.

"No," Molly said.

He pursed his lips. "I still think you're not telling me everything you know. You'd better come with me."

"You're going to lock me up?" she asked.

Timmons nodded. "Rouse is a federal officer. I don't have the authority to let you out."

"So you're going to leave me in there with your night deputy," Molly said.

"Don't worry about him," Timmons said. "His story doesn't add up. I'm going to take his badge and invite him to leave Crowheart."

"Sheriff," Molly said, "we should work together. Between the two of us, we might be able to run this killer down before he strikes again."

Timmons exhaled. His face was drawn by fatigue that was both physical and emotional. "I don't know, Miss Owens. I'll have to think on it."

Molly did not resist as Sheriff Timmons took her back to the cell. After she was locked inside, she heard raised voices coming from the office at the end of the corridor. Timmons and the night deputy were engaged in a shouting match. Then a door slammed shut, followed by silence.

Later Molly heard several excited voices and overheard enough to know that Timmons had summoned help to move the body of Jack McGrath. She heard him tell someone to take it to the makeshift mortuary in the back of a nearby furniture and cabinetmaker's shop.

Molly stretched out on the bunk and closed her eyes. Two hours past daybreak she was awakened by a key rattling in the door lock. She sat up and saw a sleepy-eyed Sheriff Timmons opening the barred door.

"Rouse is dropping the charge against you," he said.

Molly swung her feet down and stood. "Did he say why?"

"Claimed he was too busy to go to Cheyenne and prosecute you," Timmons said, stepping aside as Molly came out of the cell. "He figures a night in jail will be enough to keep you from trespassing on the reservation again."

Molly looked at him. "Did you tell him—"

"No," Timmons interrupted, "I never let on who you are, and I don't aim to tell anyone you discovered the body. Folks are going to be hopping mad when they find out about the killing, and if word gets around how you escaped, I'd be run out of Crowheart, likely." He added, "And I'm not ready to leave town."

"Sheriff," Molly said, "let's work together."

Timmons nodded. "Hell, I'm no investigator. I've got my hands full serving papers and keeping the peace." He held out his hand to shake. "I need your help."

Molly grasped his hand. "I have some leads to follow. I'll keep you up-to-date on my investigation."

"You be careful now," he said with a tired smile.

"I will," Molly said. "There is one thing you can do for me."

"What's that?" he asked.

"Keep an eye on Rouse whenever you have a chance," Molly said.

Timmons was surprised. "You figure he's mixed up in this thing?"

"I don't know," Molly said, "but I think someone is withholding government allotments from the Shoshones."

Timmons whistled softly. "But that doesn't make him a murderer."

Molly nodded agreement. "I don't know how the pieces of this puzzle fit together, but I have a couple of ideas. What I need now is the proof."

"I see," Timmons said. "Well, I hope you don't plan any more rides onto the reservation. Next time, Rouse or Stobaugh will have you locked up for good."

"I'm going to work on that problem," Molly said, moving down the corridor, "as soon as I leave here."

Before riding out of Crowheart, Molly telegraphed an urgent message to Horace Fenton in which she requested authorization from General Holcomb to enter Indian lands. She still believed Eagle-in-Flight held the key to identifying Isaiah Holcomb's murderer, and she wanted to go back to the reservation as soon as possible. But she preferred to make the next trip with the army's blessing.

Molly spent much of the next three days riding Pitchfork range during fall roundup. Cowhands mounted on agile cutting horses separated the mature three-year-olds from the milling herds of cattle. Then began the slow work of driving those critters to a common point in the southeast sector of the ranch. From there the steers would be herded to railroad loading pens outside Crowheart for shipment to the Kansas City stockyards.

The work of separating and moving cattle was often tedious and dirty, but Molly saw beauty in it, too. Those lean men on horseback performed a dangerous ballet, with muscular quarterhorses charging and feinting, wheeling one way and a second later reversing direction, turning on a dime as the saying went, to give nine cents change.

Molly stayed clear of the cowhands while they worked, but at noontime she joined them in camp. They were congenial men who teased one another mercilessly, but maintained a formal politeness toward her. She quickly learned that the real cowhands on the Pitchfork, most of whom had been hired by Isaiah Holcomb, did not get along with the gunmen hired by Pardee. The two groups were distinct in both appearance and manner. They rarely mingled, and from bits and pieces of overheard conversations, Molly came to realize there had been fist fights in the bunkhouse between them.

Molly observed the armed riders as they patrolled the timbered foothills. From a distance she watched through her field glasses as the gunmen rode in twos and threes along the boundary of the reservation. These men were often out several days at a time, leading pack animals laden with supplies.

But since the one incident when the Shoshones had swept down from the foothills and butchered Pitchfork steers, all had been peaceful. No more Indians had been sighted.

Joe Pardee took full credit, boasting that no Indian or rustler would dare venture onto Pitchfork range. One evening on the veranda Molly overheard the foreman insist to Nell that the extra men be kept on the payroll after roundup and even later into the fall after the mature cattle had been shipped to the stockyards.

"But that will cut into our profit, Joe," Nell said.

"Yes, ma'am, it will," he said, "but that's money well spent. So long as the savages see armed riders in those hills, they'll leave us be."

"I suppose so," Nell conceded. After a moment Molly heard her say, "Do as you see fit, Joe."

"Yes, ma'am," he said, and trooped out of the house.

After breakfast the next morning Molly went to the barn and saddled her horse. As she turned to lead the big gelding out of his stall, Molly saw Pardee standing in the runway, hands on his hips.

"Stop bothering Pitchfork riders," he said.

Molly dropped the horse's reins. "What're you talking about?"

He came closer, swaying slightly. "You know damn well what I'm talking about."

Molly realized Pardee had started this day with a drink. His breath reeked of whiskey.

"Men can't keep their minds on work to be done when you're out there flirting with them," Pardee said.

"Who told you I've flirted with any man on this ranch?" Molly demanded.

"I've got eyes," he said. "I've seen you in cow camps for the last three days."

"Then you know it isn't true," Molly said. "I haven't flirted with anyone."

"Calling me a liar?" he said.

"That's right, Pardee," Molly said. "I am calling you a liar. And if you ever accuse me of flirting with the men again, I'll make sure everyone on this ranch knows you're a liar."

"If you was a man," he said, "I'd bust your face up."

Molly said, "You're welcome to try." She took a step toward him.

Obviously unprepared for her boldness, Pardee retreated.

"Last time we were alone," Molly said, "you tried to ride me down. Now that you're on foot, you're not so brave, are you?"

"Damn you," Pardee growled, doubling up his fists, "I oughta knock the sass out of you."

Molly took another step toward him. "I'm not afraid of you. Take your Sunday punch."

Cursing, he backed away. Molly closed the distance between them, daring him to carry through with his threat. Pardee swore at her again, then abruptly turned away and strode out of the barn. As the door slammed shut, Molly was startled to hear another voice.

"Damned if you didn't give him more than he bargained for."

Molly turned and peered into the shadows across the runway. A man limped out of a horse stall.

"Bud," she said.

The wrangler moved into the dusty shafts of light that filtered down through the haymow. Molly saw that he carried an axe handle.

"Thought I was going to have to club him," Bud said, "but you called his bluff and backed him down. Yes, ma'am, you did a proper job of it." He chuckled. "Joe probably figures you're aiming to take over the Pitchfork, and it's driving him wild."

"That's a rumor I'd like to get stopped," Molly said.

"Well, I'll tell you, Miss Owens," Bud said, grinning broadly, "it's a rumor the cowhands are getting a big kick out of."

CHAPTER XVIII

The sky was clear and the morning air crisp when Molly rode her buckskin gelding to Crowheart. She reached the outskirts of town just as a freight train was departing.

Bell ringing, the big steam engine pulled a line of sixteen stock and boxcars along Front Street, leaving a cloud of black smoke behind. Down a side street Molly saw an aproned woman rush out of her house to the back yard clothes line where she snatched sheets and pillow cases off the line before the settling cinders and soot from the engine's smoke stack ruined her morning wash.

Molly reined up at the train depot and dismounted. She entered the depot and crossed the waiting room to the telegraph office. The gaunt telegrapher saw her coming and pushed the green eyeshade up on his forehead. Reaching into a row of pigeonholes, he pulled out a sealed envelope and handed it to Molly as she came to the desk.

Molly turned away and tore the envelope open, quickly reading the message. Horace Fenton had worked fast. Within minutes of receiving Molly's request, he relayed it to General Holcomb. That same day Holcomb had obtained permission for her to enter Indian lands "at her own peril," and the official orders from Fort Robinson to Camp Lincoln had been sent by wire.

Molly went outside to her horse. She found an angry Nathan Rouse waiting at the tie rail. In his hand was a sheet of paper bearing a telegraphed message. He waved it at Molly.

"So you went over my head," he said. "I should never have let you out of jail."

"You should never have put me in jail, Mr. Rouse," Molly said, meeting his gaze as she untied her horse's reins.

"If you don't believe I can keep you off the reservation," he said, "then I'll prove it to you. I just wired a message to Washington. Within twenty-four hours the Indian Bureau will rescind that army order."

Molly moved to her horse's side. "Then we don't have anything to talk about, do we?"

"We have plenty to talk about," Rouse said. "I want to know what's so all-fired interesting to you on that reservation?" He gave her a once-over. "Those Indian warriors excite you more than white men? Is that it? You like to lie down on a bear rug in a tepee and take on a Shoshone—or half a dozen of them?"

Molly drew her hand back. In a swift motion she slapped him across the face, hard.

Rouse came for her, fists clenched.

Molly did not back away, but looped the reins over the saddle horn and faced him.

Rouse stopped, glaring at her. The side of his face was reddened where Molly had struck him.

"Say that again," Molly said evenly, "and I'll do more than just slap you."

Rouse blinked, then whirled and walked away, crossing Front Street toward the side street that led to his office.

Molly rode back to the Pitchfork. As she passed through the ranch gate she saw an army horse tied at the rail in front of the house. She rode to the barn and stabled her gelding. When she walked to the veranda, she found Colonel Stobaugh waiting for her.

"Colonel," Molly said in greeting. She climbed the steps, seeing an icy expression of his face.

"I don't know why you're here or what you aim to do, Miss Owens," he said. "All I know is that you're to have anything the army can provide, and you have authority to come and go on the Shoshone reservation as you please."

His voice was low and dry as he continued, "I wouldn't have believed the order if it had not come down from high command. Damnedest thing I ever heard of. But like a good soldier, I obey orders." He spoke those last words with a sense of irony in his voice.

"I won't cause you any trouble—" Molly began.

"A woman riding alone out here is trouble, Miss Owens," Stobaugh interrupted. "And who will get blamed if a Shoshone abuses you or takes your scalp? Folks around here will blame me, first. Second, they'll blame the army for failing to protect the *innocent* citizenry."

"Colonel," Molly said, "I can look out for myself."

"You can fight off a band of Shoshone warriors?" he demanded.

"What makes you think I'll be attacked?" Molly asked.

"Young warriors in that tribe are looking for trouble," Stobaugh said.

"Are they looking for trouble," Molly asked, "or food?"

"Can you back up that accusation?" he asked.

Molly briefly recounted her journey onto the reservation with Morning Star, and repeated what she had learned from Eagle-in-Flight. She did not mention the fact that the young chieftain carried Isaiah Holcomb's Winchester.

"Impossible," Stobaugh said. "That Indian was lying to you."

"Morning Star didn't think so," Molly said. "Perhaps you're being lied to."

"How so?" Stobaugh asked.

"Do you keep track of the supplies delivered to the tribe?" she askd. "Or the exact number of steers?"

"That's the responsibility of the Indian Bureau," Stobaugh said, "not the army."

"You mean, Nathan Rouse," Molly said.

Stobaugh nodded. "Rouse distributes the government allotments of supplies and food. You don't seem to understand that the army is strictly a peace-keeping force here."

"And you don't seem to understand that Eagle-in-Flight could be telling the truth," Molly said.

Stobaugh stared at her. "You're suggesting the Indian agent is lying."

"I'm suggesting that he doesn't answer to anyone closer than someone in an office in Washington, D.C.," Molly said, "and we have no way of knowing whether he's telling the truth, or not."

By his protracted silence Stobaugh conceded the point. "I can't figure you out, Miss Owens," he said at last. "You came here asking questions about the investigation into the murder of Isaiah Holcomb. Now you're talking to the Shoshones. What's your interest in tribal problems?"

"I believe the two are related," Molly said. "Isn't it true that ever since Isaiah Holcomb was murdered, the problems with Indians have worsened?"

"Why, yes," he said, "but that's a symptom of the trouble here. Some of those young warriors are out to kill whites."

Molly realized she could not explain her theory in detail without revealing more of her investigation than she wanted to. Anything she told Colonel Stobaugh might go straight to Nathan Rouse.

"Perhaps I can prove that one way or the other," Molly said, "by talking to the Shoshones. Seems to me no one is hearing their side of the story."

Stobaugh shook his head. "You can't just ride onto the reservation like a sightseer, Miss Owens. You're a woman. Carrying a saddle gun and riding straddle like a man doesn't change that."

"Colonel—" Molly began.

He waved her silent. "I don't have time to argue with you. I've been ordered to provide you with anything you need—trooper escort or anything else. Now, just what the hell do you want?"

Molly met his gaze. "From you," she said, "nothing."

Riding out at dawn the next day Molly and Morning Star left the ranch and rode into the timbered foot-hills. The bright sun was almost straight overhead when they were met by a pair of mounted warriors. Armed, the two Shoshone men listened impassively to Morning Star, and then without a word escorted them to the Shoshone encampment.

Dismounting in the circular meeting ground in the center of the village, Morning Star spoke to a white-haired old man of the tribe, and then translated his reply to Molly. Most of the warriors, including Eagle-in-Flight, were out hunting and would not return until evening.

Molly thought a moment. "We'll wait."

The afternoon passed with Molly and Morning Star exploring the camp. As Molly had observed before, everyone worked. Old men shaved and smoothed wil-lows into arrow shafts that would be fitted with feathers and points. Women tended meat and wild vegetables simmering in iron pots suspended over fires.

Other women used stone hammers to pound dried meat into a mix of wild berries and hot animal fat, making pemmican that was spooned into sections of intestine. After the ends were tied, these links made a nutritious food that would keep through the winter and protect the Shoshones from scurvy.

The women wore soft buckskin dresses that reached to their ankles, colorfully decorated with glass beads and porcupine quills. Their shiny black hair hung loosely to their shoulders. Young mothers carried infants in cradles made of hides.

Morning Star pointed out one young woman who was many months pregnant. "Wife of Eagle-in-Flight," she said.

Molly saw her duck into the young chieftain's lodge, a beautiful woman with large dark eyes, a slender nose and full lips. Despite her condition she moved gracefully. Through the open flap of the tepee Molly saw her sit down on a furry hide where a toddler played.

Two hunting parties returned to the encampment late in the afternoon, but Eagle-in-Flight was not among them. One of the hunting parties was led by Elk Bull.

Morning Star spoke to a hunter and reported to Molly that Eagle-in-Flight had traveled far in pursuit of elk and would not return until tomorrow. As Molly listened, she was aware that Elk Bull watched them, a hostile expression on his face. She did not return his baleful stare, but considered the risk of leaving here and making a night ride to the Pitchfork.

She did not know what to expect from Elk Bull, but she sensed it was safer to stay here than to ride out. She told Morning Star to make it known they would wait for Eagle-in-Flight, gambling that Elk Bull would not harm them if he knew that.

A white-haired Shoshone woman took them to a lodge behind Eagle-in-Flight's. A meal of venison stew was brought to them, along with several rusty cans of peas. Morning Star explained to Molly that these were part of an old government ration, food that the Shoshones either disliked or had never figured out what to do with.

As the evening light faded, so did the hubbub of voices, children's shouts and barking dogs. Molly and Morning Star undressed in the lodge while several giggling children peeked through the flap. Morning Star shooed them away, and then the two women crawled under heavy animal hides that were fragrant with the odor of smoke.

Outside a fire had been built in the meeting ground of the encampment. The men of the tribe gathered there. Late into the night Molly heard them talking in low voices. Something in their tone, along with the sounds of the crackling fire, had a soothing effect on Molly. She slept with her gun in hand, but closed her eyes feeling confident she would not need it.

What seemed to be only a moment later, Molly opened her eyes to bright daylight, and realized she had been lulled to sleep by those night sounds.

Morning Star was already up and dressed. She left the lodge and presently returned with a breakfast of dried trout, hardtack from the government ration, and a tin cup filled with creek water.

After the meal Molly stepped out of the lodge, blinking against the sunlight. A hint of fall was in the air that was crisp and now fragrant with the smell of many campfires. Walking about, Molly saw that the day's work had begun now that the warming sun had cleared the east horizon.

The orderly scene quickly changed to one of chaos as a volley of gunfire erupted from the line of trees on the rise overlooking this encampment. Amid shrieks and screams, Molly dove behind a lodge as bullets whispered through the air and thudded into the ground nearby.

Indian women and children ran from the gunfire toward the creek where the bank down to the water provided scant protection. Molly saw several Shoshones who were wounded. A group of screaming women ran past, followed by a boy limping after them. Blood ran from a bullet wound in his leg. An old woman lay on the ground, not moving.

A dozen men let out whoops as they sprinted toward the rise, waving guns and spears over their heads. Led by Elk Bull, they ran to confront the enemy. More shots sounded, and as Molly heard the deep boom of many rifles, she saw four warriors fall to the ground. Another screamed as a bullet tore through his shoulder. He spun around and fell. The others retreated, taking cover where they could find it behind lodges and racks of drying meat. They began firing their old rifles toward the tree line.

Molly edged back. She raised to her knees and took a deep breath. Standing, she ran. She darted between tepees and sprinted to the horses by the creek. On the ground near the milling animals, Molly saw her saddle and gear. Behind her came volley after volley of rifle fire, followed by the closer popping sounds of guns held by Shoshone warriors.

Out of the direct line of fire, Molly quickly opened her saddlebags. She pulled out her field glass case, and then snatched her Winchester out of the saddle boot. She ran back the way she had come, staying low and hiding behind tepees as much as possible.

The gunfire from the timbered rise was sporadic now that the Indians were returning fire. Many of the tepees were punctured with bullet holes, and Molly saw a cast iron pot suspended over a fire that had been cracked by a bullet. Soupy liquid seeped out, dripping into the fire where it hissed and sent up smoke and steam.

Molly halted behind a lodge on the outer perimeter of the encampment. Edging around it, she brought the field glasses to her eyes and focused on the trees. She saw riflemen lying prone there, and while she watched a man on horseback appeared between two pines.

The man wore a brown Stetson and rode a gray horse. Molly could not identify him from this distance, but now felt certain the encampment was not under attack by soldiers. It had occurred to her that Eagle-in-Flight's "hunting party" may actually have been a raiding party, and the attackers must be soldiers who had come to punish the tribe.

Molly set the field glasses down and picked up her Winchester. Taking a sitting position at the edge of the tepee, she braced her elbows on her knees and aimed the long-barreled rifle at the horsemen. Taking the distance into account, she squeezed the trigger.

A puff of dust at the feet of the gray horse told her that she had estimated the distance accurately. She jacked in a fresh round and fired again, and the prancing horse reared. She moved the sights to one side and fired again and again, unleashing her own volley on the attackers.

When the rifle was empty, she picked up her field glasses and saw men scampering away. The horse-backer up there waved vigorously at them to retreat.

In the ensuing silence the Shoshone warriors soon realized what was happening. They ran for their ponies. Molly stood, and moments later saw the warriors galloping across the basin toward the rise.

Molly headed back into the village, and found Morning Star tending the wounded near the creek bank. She knelt down and helped, hearing the cries of terrified children and the sobs of women.

Molly had not identified any of the attackers, but she had recognized the horse. That iron gray quarterhorse was ridden by Joe Pardee.

CHAPTER XIX

An old woman hobbled up to Molly and spat on her, and a teen-aged boy threw a stone that struck her arm. Molly was pushed away from a wounded woman, and she looked around to see a crowd of Indians closing in around her. The chorus of angry voices grew louder.

Morning Star stood beside Molly and screeched at the women. When one crone drew near, waving a trade knife in her hand, Morning Star kicked her and shoved her to the ground.

Morning Star turned and kicked and shoved her way through the crowd, and Molly followed her to the horses. While Morning Star held the crowd at bay by shrieking and waving her arms, Molly saddled and bridled their horses.

"Let's ride!" Molly called to her, and Morning Star turned her back to the menacing crowd and moved swiftly to the Pitchfork mare. A stone bounced off her back when she swung up to the saddle, and angry shouts followed as Molly turned her horse and splashed across the creek.

Molly spurred her horse and wind ripped past her face as the powerful animal galloped across the open basin. She heard the mare pounding close behind, and looked back to see Morning Star following. Beyond her, Molly saw the knot of Indians on the other side of the creek, still shouting taunts.

Riding through this open ground, Molly was glad that the warriors had left the encampment. She and Morning Star would have been easy targets for a Shoshone armed with a rifle.

When the lodges were out of sight, Molly reined up and slowed to a walk. Morning Star drew up beside her.

"Shoshones think you bring white men to kill them," she said.

Molly nodded. "I guessed that's what they were thinking. Can't blame them." She added, "Thanks for getting us out of there."

Morning Star smiled. "You helped me. I help you now."

Leaving the basin, Morning Star followed a well-traveled game trail through the foothills, confident that it would be safe with all the Shoshone warriors angling off to the east in pursuit of the attackers. But deep in the forest three-quarters of an hour later, she abruptly reined up, signaling Molly to do the same.

The sounds that reached Molly's ears were not identifiable at first, but after a full minute of listening she realized animals were coming down the trail behind them. The sounds she heard were of plodding horses, and now she heard the creak of saddle leather.

Molly and Morning Star quickly dismounted and led their horses off the trail, covering their tracks as they did so. They moved back into the trees where they could not be seen.

Molly peered through the boughs as the sounds became more distinct. She saw movement, and then caught a glimpse of a horseman. He rode past, followed by half a dozen pack animals, fully loaded. Two more horsemen, carrying rifles, trailed the pack train.

She was not close enough to get a clear look at any of the men, but she did not think they were part of the group that had attacked the Shoshone encampment. More likely, she thought, they were poachers or prospectors trespassing on reservation land.

Molly and Morning Star waited in the trees half an hour, then rode out, making their way through the forest and staying away from the trail. Long after sundown they topped the last foothill and saw the lamplit windows of the Pitchfork ranch.

"Promise me you won't go back there," Nell said after Molly briefly explained why she and Morning Star had stayed overnight at the Shoshone encampment. "You'll be killed next time—the both of you."

Molly smiled as Morning Star held her baby and leaned her face close to his, speaking softly.

"I'm serious, Molly," Nell said. "Times have changed, and we're going to have Indian trouble."

Molly turned to her. "We will unless someone stops it."

In the morning after breakfast Molly caught Joe Pardee as he walked out of the mess hall.

"What do you want?" he demanded, stopping as Molly stepped in front of him.

"I want to know why you and your gunmen were using Shoshones for target practice yesterday," she said.

"What?" he said in amazement.

Molly said nothing, but stared at him.

"You're a damned liar," he said.

"You were on the reservation yesterday," Molly said, "riding that gray quarterhorse of yours."

"The hell," he said. "I was riding the range all day yesterday, working cattle."

"And you've got eight or ten witnesses to back you up, don't you?" Molly said. "That's how many riflemen I counted."

"You counted," he repeated dully.

"That's right," Molly said. "I was in that encampment, dodging bullets. I looked right at you through my field glasses."

Pardee glared at her. "You've been hunting trouble ever since you got here. Well, by God, I reckon you just found it—more than you bargained for." He brushed past her as he headed for the bunkhouse, his boots scuffing dirt with every long stride.

Molly knew she could not prove her accusation in a court of law, but she was convinced she had recognized Pardee's horse yesterday and she knew he did not allow anyone else to ride it. Now she hoped to make something happen. Sufficiently angered, Pardee might do something foolish, something that would incriminate him.

Molly had decided the quickest and safest way to report the attack on the Shoshone encampment to Colonel Stobaugh was by wire. She hurried to the horse barn and saddled her gelding, then rode for town.

Several miles away from Crowheart Molly saw a line of riders on the flat expanse of grassland between the foothills and the Wind River. From their formation she realized they were soldiers, headed for town at a fast pace.

Molly spurred her horse. Leaving the ranch road, she galloped toward them. As she closed the distance, she saw that the detachment was led by a tall officer who rode straight-backed in his McClellan saddle. He was Colonel Stobaugh.

A shout from a trooper alerted Stobaugh to Molly's approach. He swung away from the detachment, waved the men on, and rode out to meet Molly. He was dressed in full uniform and wore a saber at his side.

Molly reined up. "Looks like you're in a hurry, colonel."

Stobaugh nodded curtly. "A Shoshone raiding party hit Crowheart at dawn."

"What happened?" Molly asked.

"According to the message that came over our wire in HQ," Stobaugh said, "Indians set fire to several houses and shot at the people who ran out." He glanced toward the double line of mounted troopers moving south. "We'll pick up the trail of that raiding party and run them down. They need to be taught a lesson, looks like."

"They were replying in kind, colonel," Molly said.

"What do you mean?" he asked.

Molly briefly recounted what she had seen yesterday at the Shoshone encampment. "I'm certain the attackers were led by Joe Pardee, and they must have been the gunmen he hired a while back."

"Will you swear to that in court?" Stobaugh asked.

"I'll swear to what I saw," she said.

Stobaugh studied her, then glanced over his shoulder again. "We'll have to talk about this later." He turned his horse.

"I'm coming with you," Molly said.

"This is military business," Stobaugh said over his shoulder.

"I'm headed for Crowheart," Molly said. "I can ride with you, or behind you."

The colonel shot an annoyed look at her, but then his expression softened to resignation. "All right. If you can keep up, come on."

Molly's gelding was stronger than any horse wearing a U.S. government brand, and she had no trouble holding the pace. The detachment reached Crowheart before noon. On the north edge of town Molly saw the charred remains of three houses. Frameworks of walls stood like blackened skeletons, and thin lines of smoke rose up from charred timbers.

The arrival of the troopers drew a crowd of angry townspeople. Many of the men were armed with rifles or shotguns and were ready to ride. Stobaugh sent his scouts out to pick up the Shoshones' trail, and then spoke to the armed men. Molly heard him say that much as he appreciated their offer to help, the army did not need civilian aid.

"I expect to run down that raiding party by dark," Stobaugh said.

"Shoot those savages!" said a man holding a double-barreled shotgun. "Shoot 'em like they shot at our women and children!"

Angry shouts came from the crowd as threats of revenge were made. No one had been killed here this morning, but two women and a boy had been wounded. Molly could see the people were scared and angry, much like the Indian women who had driven her out of the Shoshone encampment yesterday.

A captain rode up to Colonel Stobaugh. Molly was close enough to hear his report: Troopers making a sweep on the grassland outside of town had cut the trail of unshod ponies.

Stobaugh swung his horse around and was about to ride out with the captain when he was hailed by a man on horseback galloping up the street. Molly turned to see Nathan Rouse waving at the colonel.

The Indian agent drew up, cast a severe glance at Molly, and spoke to the colonel. "When you're ready to pursue the Shoshones, I'll ride with you."

Stobaugh nodded. "We're moving out right now."

"Then let's get on with it," Rouse said, giving the brim of his bowler a tug.

As they spurred their horses and cantered away, Molly let up on the reins. Her horse followed the troopers. Stobaugh had ridden only fifty yards when he looked back and saw her at the rear of the detachment. He turned his horse and came back to her.

"Miss Owens," he said, raising a gloved hand, "this is the end of the line for you. Those Shoshones are in a fighting mood—"

"And you'll need a peacemaker," Molly interrupted.

"What?" Stobaugh asked.

"I've been on the reservation twice," Molly said. "Both Eagle-in-Flight and Elk Bull know me. I can be of help to you."

Stobaugh shook his head. "I'll have to get along without you."

"Then I'll follow the trail myself," Molly said. "I told you why those Indians are angry. They shouldn't be shot down like mad dogs."

"That isn't my intention, Miss Owens," he said.

"But if we don't try to make peace—"

"Damn it, I don't have time to sit here and argue," Stobaugh said. He wheeled his horse around and dug in his spurs.

Molly took that to mean he would not prevent her from accompanying the detachment, and rode after him.

CHAPTER XX

The dim trail of unshod ponies led through the wide sweep of grasslands toward the timbered foothills and the Owl Mountains, straight to the nearest boundary of the Shoshone reservation.

Molly rode alone at the rear of the column, and soon after leaving Crowheart she had tied a handkerchief around her mouth and nose to filter out the haze of dust stirred up by thirty trotting army horses. The soldiers rode in pairs, flanked by their officers. At the head of the column Nathan Rouse rode beside Colonel Stobaugh, and one hundred yards ahead of them a pair of scouts kept sight of the trail, watching for trouble to their front.

Molly had seen Rouse look back at her as the detachment marched away from the burned houses in Crowheart. She saw him confer intently with Stobaugh, obviously complaining about her presence. Stobaugh acknowledged the Indian agent's point with a shrug and replied with a brief shake of his head.

Upon reaching the timbered foothills Stobaugh brought his detachment to a halt. He gathered his officers about him, a captain and two lieutenants, and they in turn sent half a dozen men from the ranks ahead to act as scouts. The main body of troopers dismounted for a rest and the noon meal of hardtack, beans, and jerked beef.

Molly tended her horse and then took her canteen as she moved away a short distance and reclined in the high grass. The grass was cool and fragrant. She listened to the voices of the soldiers and heard them breaking out their rations while she looked up at fluffy cumulus clouds, aware that many of the men stole glances at her.

She turned her head and saw Colonel Stobaugh leave his officers and Nathan Rouse to bring her a full ration of food. Molly raised up on an elbow as he approached.

"Here's some food," he said, kneeling beside her.

"Lun Sing filled me up with a cowhand's breakfast of steak and eggs," Molly said. "No need for me to take food meant for your troopers."

"Nonsense," Stobaugh said, holding a hard biscuit and strip of dark red beef out to her. "We always carry extra rations. I insist you eat while you're riding with me."

Molly smiled at him and accepted the food. "I appreciate your willingness to let me ride with you. I guess not everyone here is pleased with your decision."

"Troopers like nothing better than to have a woman around," he said. "Rouse is the only one who complained."

"I'm not surprised," Molly said.

"You think he's a crook, don't you?" Stobaugh said.

Molly nodded, meeting his gaze. "What do you think of the man, colonel?"

Stobaugh looked away from her. For a long moment he studied the grassland they had just crossed. "Since you raised the question with me, I've had second thoughts about him. I think an investigation is in order. When the dust settles, I'm going to recommend that to high command."

His gaze came back to her. "I've had second thoughts about you, too."

"Why, colonel," Molly said with a quick smile.

Stobaugh's face reddened. "What I mean is . . . " His voice trailed off, and he cleared his throat. "I mean I was short with you at the Pitchfork, and I regret it. I've come to the conclusion that you're here for more than just a visit. You've come to do a job, and you have some powerful friends to help you. One of them must be General Zachary Holcomb."

"Interesting theory," Molly said.

"Holcomb has to be the one who obtained authorization for you to enter Shoshone lands," Stobaugh said. "Now that I've thought about it, I reckon I'd have done the same thing if I were in his boots. The investigation into Isaiah's murder was at a standstill before you got here. Time to bring in outside help." He asked, "Is my theory correct?"

Molly paused before answering. "All I can tell you, colonel, is that I hope you'll keep your theory to yourself."

A brief smile crossed his face. "I will."

The strategy of the retreating Shoshones became apparent upon the return of the scouts. The raiding party had divided in the forest. Singly or in pairs the Indians had ridden off in separate directions, probably agreeing to meet at a distant point. Following all of them was an impossible task, and tracking a pair of Shoshones through the forest here would be difficult at best.

Molly watched Stobaugh as he formulated his decision. First, he sent two riders back to Camp Lincoln for reinforcements; then he announced his plan to the gathered troopers. They would ride straight to the main Shoshone encampment where the fresh troopers would meet them. The encampment would be encircled and searched. If no warriors were found there, particularly Eagle-in-Flight or Elk Bull, then prisoners would be taken and held at Camp Lincoln in an attempt to lure the raiding party out of hiding.

Enthused by this plan of direct action against the Indians, the troopers who for months had been confined to patrol duty now swiftly moved to their horses, tightened saddle cinches and mounted.

"Better leave the woman behind," Rouse said in a loud voice. He stood beside his horse, holding the reins.

Stobaugh had just swung up. He turned in the saddle and looked down at the Indian agent. "Mr.

Rouse, I give the orders here. Would you care to return to Crowheart?"

Rouse's face turned red as he met the colonel's gaze. "Is that an order?"

"It's an opportunity," Stobaugh replied.

"Then I'll decline it," the Indian agent said. He thrust a boot into his stirrup and mounted.

Stobaugh's command to move out was issued by the ranking sergeant, and Molly followed as the detachment rode into the cool shadows of the pine forest covering the slope of the foothill.

The excitement of this morning's chase was now replaced by mounting anticipation. Molly sensed the mood of the men changing as they rode through the trees, single file now, peering about in search of any sign of ambush. The troopers rarely spoke to one another, but in their exchange of glances was a certainty that battle was ahead.

The route through the forest took the detachment over the first ridge and down into the meadow where Isaiah Holcomb had been murdered. After watering horses in the pond there, Stobaugh led the way into the trees and over the next foothill in a direction that would take them to the great basin.

Molly rode out of the meadow with a sense of doom. The dark mood came partly from the unexpected reminder of the murder she had come here to solve, and partly from her realization that these soldiers were eager for combat.

In a way she could not blame them. These men were trained to fight, and taught that the Indians were an enemy who must be defeated. Never mind that the Shoshones had already been defeated—a defeat marked by the abandonment of Fort Laramie five years ago—and their nomadic way of life taken from them when they were caged in a reservation. The fighting men who arrived for duty at Camp Lincoln came to find their orders were simply to guard boundaries and keep the peace between red men and white.

Molly knew the Shoshones would fight, and she knew they would be outgunned. An attack by Stobaugh's soldiers would be murderous.

At mid-afternoon the column halted. Far back at the end of the line, Molly was unable to see through the growth of pine trees ahead, but she had judged the riding time by the sun and knew the basin holding the Shoshone encampment was not far away. Men and horses waited quietly in the cool shadows of the forest while a pair of scouts went ahead on foot. In twenty minutes they returned.

Molly heard their voices. The men spoke louder than she expected, but she was too far away to understand all that was said.

Presently the troopers rode forward, Springfields braced on their thighs, and moved out of the forest in a line. The basin was just ahead. Molly came out of the trees at the top of the rise overlooking it. She quickly understood why Stobaugh had made no effort to spread the detachment out into a formation that would encircle the encampment.

In the meadow below Molly saw only blackened fire rings and bare ground where more than two hundred lodges had stood night before last. The Shoshones were gone.

CHAPTER XXI

"They haven't had time to travel far from here," Colonel Stobaugh said. "Tracking women and children should not be difficult."

Molly overheard this remark as she rode past the waiting soldiers to the small rise in the terrain where the officers and Nathan Rouse gathered around Stobaugh. This was the rise that overlooked the site of the Shoshone encampment and commanded the whole basin.

"The savages may have retreated into those mountains, sir," the captain said as he gazed at the high snowy peaks beyond the basin. Molly glanced at him. He was an intense young man with blue eyes, a long thin nose, and a drooping mustache that made him look older than he was, and sadder.

"No, no," Rouse said with an impatient edge to his voice. "The Owl Mountains are sacred ground to the Shoshones. They're too superstitious to go into that country."

Stobaugh looked around, surveying the basin from one forested side to the other. "Maybe they got a new message from a medicine man, and decided it was time to hide out in those mountain valleys."

"I assure you, colonel," Rouse said, "you won't find any Indians there." He raised an arm, gesturing to the forest. "The Shoshone know how to disappear in this country. They'll divide into small bands and head into the timber like a herd of elk. No sense in wasting time by hunting for them in the Owls."

Stobaugh regarded the Indian agent for several moments, and then turned his attention to the officers at his side. "Send your best scouts down there. We'll wait here for the troopers from Lincoln. In the meantime maybe we can cut enough sign to find out if Mr. Rouse is correct."

Molly dismounted and led her horse into the shade of the pine trees. Taking her canteen from the saddle horn, she sat down nearby and watched the troopers dismount. Half a dozen of them, led by the captain, left the bivouacked detachment and rode down the slope toward the black fire rings that marked the site of the Shoshone village.

Less than an hour later the troopers from Camp Lincoln arrived, entering the basin from the south. Led by a young lieutenant, the forty men sighted the mirror signal from Colonel Stobaugh and joined the detachment overlooking the flat-bottomed basin. Stobaugh briefed the lieutenant as the men dismounted, slapped dust off their hats, and moved into cool shade with the other troopers.

The scouts soon returned, and Molly got to her feet and walked out to the officers to hear what the captain reported. She saw a self-satisfied smile on Rouse's face. Many tracks and travois marks had been found, leading in all directions except toward the Owl Mountains.

After dividing the troopers into three groups, Stobaugh deployed them. The first, under command of the captain, rode south. The second group would be led to the north end of the basin by the ranking lieutenant. Stobaugh assumed command of the third group himself, and took a middle ground. He would search the forest land here while listening for gunfire from the north or the south. His men could lend support in either direction if needed. At nightfall all three groups would return to the site of the Shoshone encampment.

As the troopers rode out, Molly saw Nathan Rouse take Colonel Stobaugh aside. She watched them turn their backs to her and confer, sensing that she was the subject under discussion.

Both men turned their horses and rode to her.

"You can ride back to the Pitchfork, Miss Owens," Stobaugh said. "I'll pull a couple men off the line to escort you."

"Thanks for the offer, colonel," Molly said, "but I want to see this thing through. I'll ride with you."

Rouse scowled, watching the colonel's face for a sign of what his reply would be.

"All right, then," Stobaugh said, "you may continue at your own risk—"

"Damn it, colonel," Rouse interrupted, "these savages are whipped up and ready to fight down to the last woman and child. Nursemaiding this Indian lover just adds another problem."

"Mr. Rouse," Colonel Stobaugh said darkly, "you may stand here and apologize to the lady for that remark, or you may leave us—immediately."

"I'll leave," he said. "I'll ride out with your captain." With a note of defiance, he added, "Need I remind you who'll get blamed if she takes an arrow, or worse, gets captured?"

"I have no doubt you'll see to it that the right man is blamed, Mr. Rouse," Stobaugh replied.

The Indian agent reined his horse around and galloped away to join the squad of troopers heading north under command of the captain.

Stobaugh watched him go, then turned and gestured to the butt of the Winchester in Molly's saddle boot. "Stay close to my men, and be prepared to use that weapon. For all of his faults, Rouse is probably correct in his assessment of the Shoshones' mood."

But this time Rouse was wrong. Scouts under Stobaugh's command quickly found tracks left by ponies pulling travois. Following this trail across the basin and into the pines soon brought the troopers to a clearing where four families, minus their men, were camped. Tepees still rolled up on travois, the women and children huddled around a campfire as the troopers rode into the clearing, rifles cocked and held at the ready.

With sign language and sweeping gestures, the troopers made it known the Indians were prisoners now and must return to the basin. Molly watched as the women packed their belongings, loaded up their travois, and marched out of the clearing in ragtag fashion with their trooper escort.

By the end of the day nearly a hundred Shoshone women and children had been herded together on the creek bank near the sight of their original encampment. Among them, Molly noticed, was the pregnant wife of Eagle-in-Flight. She sat serenely, holding her toddler. The child's dark eyes darted about, wide with fear.

Not one warrior was captured. None of the three squads had caught sight of Shoshone men, much less pursued them.

"You can bet they're out there," Rouse said loudly. "They'll hit us tonight or tomorrow."

"We'll be ready," Colonel Stobaugh said, casting a critical look at the Indian agent.

Dead timber was dragged out of the forest and used to build a breastworks around the perimeter of camp. A bonfire in the middle was fueled to burn all night on the theory that the warriors would not attack when they could see the position was heavily guarded and their own women and children would be endangered.

Molly had picketed her gelding with the army horses and carried her saddle and gear to a campsite she'd found in the high grass. She was close enough to the soldiers' bedding ground to be safe, yet far enough away for privacy.

Stobaugh brought rations to her, along with steaming coffee in a tin cup. He knelt beside her, looking back at the bivouac and the huddled prisoners now lighted by leaping flames from the nearby bonfire.

"Maybe the warriors won't fight," she said, chewing a bite of hardtack softened by the hot coffee. "Eagle-in-Flight made his point in Crowheart this morning."

The side of Stobaugh's face shone in the firelight as he turned to look at Molly. "Could be." He added, "Rouse has my men nervous as cats, though. He claims the Shoshone men are crazed by the warrior spirit, and won't be satisfied until they've done battle."

"I have a higher regard for the Shoshones than Nathan Rouse does," Molly said. "The Indians are angry, and they have a right to be. The people of Crowheart feel the same way now that they've been attacked."

Under the starry night sky Molly lay wrapped in an army blanket with her head on her saddle and her Winchester at her side. A live round was in the chamber. She slept fitfully, awakening to the loud popping and crackling of the bonfire to see shadowy figures of troopers walking guard duty. Along with the others, she awaited the attack that never came.

At the first hint of light in the eastern sky, she left her bed in the grass and went to the creek, feeling groggy from lack of sleep. Cold water splashed on her face revived her somewhat, and when she returned to the bonfire a trooper brought her a tin cup filled with coffee. She drank it, watching the sky turn pink. Soon the morning quiet was broken by the rough voices of sergeants issuing commands to the waking troopers.

After the troopers and Indians were fed, and horses saddled, Stobaugh told Nathan Rouse to give the order of the day to the prisoners: They would walk to Camp Lincoln.

Molly saw consternation in the faces of the Indians as they listened to Rouse bark out Shoshone words. Some of the old women began to wail, and fearful children cried.

Angry, Rouse shouted at the women until they quieted. Mothers silenced their children. Molly saw their expressions harden as mounted troopers moved in a line toward them, herding them like animals. No one resisted. They hurriedly picked up their belongings, lashed travois poles to ponies that exhaled steam into the chill morning air, and began walking toward the trees at the south edge of the basin.

Molly rode behind as half the troopers made a formation at the rear and the other half, led by Colonel Stobaugh, moved slowly toward a break in the forest. That break marked the trail to Camp Lincoln, a trial that had been widened over the years by wagon traffic delivering government supplies.

Upon entering the forest, the formation strung out in a rough line. This long line of Indians on foot and troopers on horseback had traveled into the trees only two hundred yards when gunfire exploded, followed by panicked shouts.

"Ambush!" came the call down the line. "Ambush!"

CHAPTER XXII

From her position at the rear of the column Molly was the last to know what was happening, but the moment gunfire thundered from the dense growth of trees and arrows whispered through the air, she slid out of the saddle and grasped her horse's reins at the bit.

Ahead she saw horses rearing amid shouted curses, and then came loud reports of Springfield rifles. The troopers fought to control their terrified mounts and return fire at the same time. Hats sailed to the ground, and wounded men cried out in agony as they tumbled from their saddles.

Molly saw one trooper go down when a feathered arrow pierced his neck. Another was shot through the chest. Rifle falling from his hands, the man fell silently to the trail where he lay still.

Molly backed her horse off the trail while the confused battle raged. From the protection of a pine she looked ahead and saw Shoshone women and children lying flat on the ground. A pall of acrid powder smoke drifted through the shafts of sunlight coming through the trees. Molly now realized that the warriors had attacked from the east so the troopers would be blinded by the sun when they took aim.

Over the booming sounds of gunfire Molly heard the voices of sergeants shouting orders. They tried to group their men so their superior firepower could be concentrated and used to overwhelm the enemy.

But the troopers were still in disarray when Shoshone warriors, stripped and painted for war, swept out of the trees and attacked the mounted troopers with spears and knives. Molly saw more troopers spill out of their saddles under the onslaught, and the cries of the wounded grew louder.

Several women and children got to their feet and ran into the trees. The warriors engaged the troopers quickly, and left them behind as they sprinted into the forest on the other side of the trail. As suddenly as the ambush began, it ended.

"Cease firing! Reload weapons! Stand ready!"

In the silence that followed, a strange silence punctuated by groans of the wounded, Molly heard a sound behind her. Whirling around, she saw a pair of figures standing between two pines, and a long moment passed while they regarded one another.

Eagle-in-Flight stood beside his wife, one muscular arm around her shoulders. She held their toddler, and all three stared at Molly. The young chieftain's face bore thick lines of white warpaint beneath his eyes, and his fierce gaze was fixed on Molly. He held Isaiah Holcomb's Winchester in his hands.

Eagle-in-Flight touched his wife, and they turned away. Molly watched as they disappeared, swallowed by the shadows of the forest.

Molly took a deep breath, and the cries of the wounded seeped back into her consciousness. As she turned around to face the tragedy before her, she sensed that she would never forget the moment that had just passed, that she would always wonder what it meant and why it happened.

After tying her horse, Molly made her way through the jumble of soldiers and gear and dead or dying horses scattered on the trail. Wounded troopers were tended by their comrades. Molly saw several who lay still, caught in the awkward, twisted positions of death.

She saw that few Shoshone women and children had been recaptured. She walked past the crouching prisoners, and then up at the head of the column she saw that Colonel Stobaugh was down.

His face was ashen. Molly rushed to him and saw the feathered end of an arrow protruding from his hip. A lieutenant knelt beside him, cutting away his trousers with a pocket knife.

The captain stood nearby, speaking intently to the ranking sergeant, a burly Irishman with blood on his hands and sleeves. He had evidently been tending the wounded until summoned by the captain.

"Go . . . go after . . . them," Stobaugh said in a weak voice.

The captain looked down at him. "I am, sir. Sergeant O'Hara will take the detachment to Lincoln. I'll ride out with as many able-bodied men as I can assemble, and we'll run the bastards down."

Stobaugh nodded and closed his eyes. Molly knelt beside him and comforted him while the lieutenant probed the wound with the knife blade. Stobaugh passed out when the lieutenant cut flesh and extracted the flint-tipped arrow.

Molly saw the captain ride out with eighteen men who had come through the ambush unhurt. They had resupplied themselves with ammunition from their fallen comrades. Nathan Rouse rode with them.

"We're moving out!" the sergeant shouted. "Move them injuns along! We're moving out!"

The wounded were bandaged and slung over horses. So was Colonel Stobaugh, and now the ranking lieutenant took command. Molly hurried back to the end of the column and untied her horse.

She swung up into the saddle and rode up beside a wounded trooper. She reached out and grasped his arm, steadying him as the column began to move. The dead were left behind.

In Camp Lincoln that evening the wounded were tended by the camp surgeon and his assistant. Gaping wounds in more than a dozen troopers were cleansed and bandaged again. Stobaugh revived, and was given brandy while the surgeon worked on him. Molly heard the surgeon declare that sleep and rest were the best medicine for him, and when a clean bandage was secured around his upper leg, he was carried into the officers' quarters by a pair of troopers.

The captured women and children were set up in camp behind the tents, and guarded by troopers. Out of the original one hundred prisoners, less than twenty-five were brought here.

Sleep and rest were the medicine Molly needed, too. Lack of sleep last night suddenly caught up with her as she stood in the parade ground amid the wounded men, and she nearly fell asleep on her feet. The company clerk showed her to a small bedroom in HQ reserved for visiting dignitaries.

Molly undressed and fell asleep almost the moment her head hit the pillow. She slept all evening and through the night, awakened at sunrise by the bugle call for Reveille and Assembly. But even then she did not leave the bunk. She rolled over and slept soundly until mid-morning.

She was awakened by the sounds of horses and men outside. She sat up, realizing she had heard the voice of Nathan Rouse. The troopers had come in with prisoners. She heard the name "Eagle-in-Flight."

Molly hurriedly pinned up her hair, dressed, and grabbed her Stetson as she rushed out of the bedroom to the front porch of HQ. She paused there, then moved slowly out to the flagpole.

On the parade ground were the mounted troopers who had survived the ambush yesterday. They surrounded a group of bedraggled Shoshone warriors. Some were wounded and slumped to the ground.

Eagle-in-Flight stood among the unhurt warriors. Arms folded across his bare chest, he held his head high as he stared at the far mountains, as though drawing strength from sacred lands.

Molly saw Nathan Rouse ride around the bunched troopers and join the captain who was issuing orders to Sergeant O'Hara. A moment later she heard uneven footfalls behind her and turned to see Colonel Stobaugh limp out onto the porch.

The captain saw him, too, and swung down from his saddle. He strode past Molly and reported to the colonel with a crisp salute.

Molly was near enough to hear their voices, but not their words. When the captain finished, he turned and called out to a corporal.

The corporal rode forward, reaching behind his saddle as he reined up in front of HQ. He pulled out a Winchester and tossed it down. The captain caught the rifle and held it out to Stobaugh.

Molly watched as the colonel studied the tooled frame of the Winchester, and then looked past the captain, his eyes meeting hers.

"Looks like we've got your murderer, Miss Owens," he said. He held the rifle out. "This belonged to Mr. Holcomb, and was taken from that Indian out there, Eagle-in-Flight."

Behind her, Rouse spoke up. "You can bet that crazed Indian killed Jack McGrath, too."

"Can you prove that, Mr. Rouse?" Molly asked, seeing that the Indian agent had dismounted and now moved toward the flagpole.

"What more proof do we need?" he demanded.

Molly looked at Stobaugh. "Eagle-in-Flight took that Winchester from Isaiah Holcomb," she said, "after he was murdered."

"Ridiculous," Rouse said.

"Can you answer your own question?" Colonel Stobaugh said to Molly. "Can you prove your contention?"

"No," Molly said, "but I believe Eagle-in-Flight can. I'm convinced he witnessed the murder."

Rouse swore and said in a low voice, "Indian-loving bitch."

"That sort of language will not be tolerated in the presence of a lady, Mr. Rouse," Stobaugh said.

"Some lady," Rouse said.

"I think we'd better discuss this in my office, Miss Owens," Colonel Stobaugh said, casting a hard look at Rouse.

The Indian agent turned away, muttering that he had to wash off the trail dust and rinse a foul taste out of his mouth.

In his office Stobaugh grimaced as he sat on the corner of his desk, keeping weight off his injured leg. "You were not surprised to see that Winchester, were you?" He paused. "I can only presume you knew Eagle-in-Flight was carrying it."

Molly nodded. "I knew."

"And you failed to report it to me," he said.

"Eagle-in-Flight told me through an interpretor that he had taken the gun from Isaiah Holcomb's body," Molly said. "He said the killing was white man's business, and that he'd seen it."

"Did he name the killer?" Stobaugh asked.

"No," Molly said. "But I believe he will when he realizes he may be blamed for the murder."

"There's no 'may be' about it, Miss Owens," Stobaugh said. "When word gets out, folks in Crowheart will be hollering for the lynch rope." He studied Molly. "Naming the killer at this point may not make much difference in the outcome. I don't have to tell you what will happen if this comes down to Eagle-in-Flight's word against a white man's."

"You don't have to tell me," Molly said. "That's the reason I'm continuing my investigation. I need more evidence."

Stobaugh pursed his lips. "Miss Owens, I must tell you that I think you're on a blind trail. I don't know if Eagle-in-Flight himself murdered Isaiah Holcomb, but everything points to the Shoshones."

"All the circumstantial evidence, perhaps," Molly said. "But that leaves a larger question. Who had the most to gain by the death of Isaiah Holcomb?"

"I don't know the answer to that one," Stobaugh replied.

"I don't, either," Molly said. "All I know is that the Shoshones lost a friend the day he was murdered."

CHAPTER XXIII

Molly brought the news to Nell, telling her of the Winchester rifle as she recounted all that had happened during the last forty-eight hours.

"I do believe the Shoshones have gone loco," Nell said. "Joe thinks they'll try to burn us out next. He's had all the men out on patrol ever since those houses were burned in Crowheart. Molly, I'm scared. For the first time in my life out here on the Pitchfork, I'm scared."

Molly leaned forward in the elk antler chair by the fireplace and grasped Nell's bony hand. "The army has scattered the Indians and captured several warriors. The rest are hiding. You have nothing to fear." But she could see from the old woman's expression that she was deeply troubled.

"I'm thinking about giving up this ranch," Nell said. "I thought I could run it, but now I think I'm too old. Everything's changed since Isaiah died. . . ."

"You once told me you wanted to live out your days here," Molly said.

"Well, I do," she said, looking fondly around the big room. "This is home. Isaiah and I built this place . . . and now I have a grave to tend. One day I want to be buried beside him."

She was interrupted by the cooing of the baby in the next room, and she smiled. "You know, Molly, taking care of that baby has been good medicine for me. I get a lot of joy out of him—and he gets me out of this chair several times a day, I tell you."

Molly squeezed her hand. "You can do anything you put your mind to, Nell. And if you decide to run this ranch, you'll find a way to do it."

132

Nell smiled at her. "Takes a young woman to say that." She added, "You know, I wish you *were* my cousin."

Molly laughed softly.

Nell's smile faded. "But I have to face facts, and maybe the time has come for me to leave the Pitch-fork."

"Has someone offered to buy you out?" Molly asked.

Nell nodded.

"Who?" Molly asked.

"Joe," she replied.

Molly was surprised to hear that name.

"Oh, I know Joe would take good care of the place," Nell said.

"It's none of my business," Molly said, "but how can a man on foreman's wages afford to buy one of the best cattle ranches in Wyoming?"

"Joe told me he has an investor," Nell said. "The down payment will be enough that I can retire without a care in the world."

"Is that what you want?" Molly asked.

Nell looked at her. "No," she said at last. "I want to have cares in this world."

"Who is the investor?" Molly asked.

"I don't know," Nell said. "Joe promised to tell me all the details once I've made my decision." She looked around the room again, and a wistful expression came into her eyes as though talking to Molly about leaving this ranch house made it more real than before.

In the morning after breakfast Molly watched from the dining room window as Pardee sent his gunmen out on patrol. A few minutes ago he had told Nell that he planned to take the rest of the men with him and move a herd to new pasture—pasture that was farther away from the reservation boundary.

"No sense in making it easy for those savages to raid our stock," he had said.

"Are you leaving a few men here, Joe?" Nell asked.

"Yes, ma'am," he said, "you'll be well guarded."

But after Pardee gave the cowhands their assignments and sent them out, Molly watched from the ranch house and the foreman rode alone through the gate and followed the road to Crowheart.

Molly grabbed her Stetson and handbag and hurried out to the horse barn. She saddled her gelding and made a hard ride. Half an hour away from the ranch she saw an iron gray quarterhorse trotting along the road ahead, and reined up.

She pulled out her field glasses and focused on the rider. She had closed the distance. Pardee was headed for town.

Following at a safe distance, Molly's long-legged gelding easily kept pace with Pardee's mount. She kept sight of him through the gently rolling grasslands until the buildings of Crowheart came in sight.

Pardee swung off the main road and entered town through a back street. Molly trailed him past the Victorian homes along a tree-lined avenue to the side street where the frame building housing the Indian Bureau office of Nathan Rouse stood.

Molly tied her horse a block away and walked along the boardwalk in front of residences toward the office building. She had glimpsed Pardee as he climbed the outside staircase to the door of Rouse's office. No windows were on this side of the building, and Molly walked to the base of the staircase where Pardee's horse was tied, confident that she had not been seen. Now as she looked up at the landing, she made a quick decision.

Moving swiftly, she gingerly climbed the steps on tiptoe, remembering that she had been warned by a creaking board when Jack McGrath had discovered her in Rouse's office. She grasped the bannister and walked along the edge of the steps where they were nailed, hoping that one of these boards creaked in the middle and not the edge.

She was right. She reached the landing without making a sound. Glancing down at the street behind her, she saw no one. She knelt down and put her ear to the keyhole.

Molly heard droning voices, first Pardee's and then Rouse spoke. She caught only scattered words, not the sense of what the two men were saying to one another. Moments later she heard footfalls on the floor in there, and Rouse's voice grew louder just as the door handle rattled and turned.

Molly quickly raised up and stepped to the far side of the landing, pressing against the clapboard wall just as the door swung out. Her view was blocked for several seconds, but then the door was pulled shut and she saw Pardee descending the stairs.

Molly held her breath as Pardee reached the board-walk. He turned and untied the reins of his horse. He seemed ready to look back the way he had come, but then he thrust a boot in his stirrup and mounted. Molly exhaled as he reined his horse around and rode out.

She quickly tiptoed down the steps and hurried down the block to her horse. She had heard only a few words and phrases the instant before the door opened, but two spoken by Rouse were enough: "Don't worry, Joe," and "gold mine."

Molly rode to Front Street, paused at the corner while a pair of farm wagons rumbled past, and headed for the sheriff's office. Half a block away she saw Timmons come out his door and start down the boardwalk in the opposite direction.

"Sheriff!" Molly called.

He turned and came back as Molly drew up at the hitching rail in front of the jailhouse.

"I'd like to talk to you," Molly said, "if you can spare a few minutes."

"I have a job in front of me right now," he replied. "Can you make this quick?"

Molly heard an icy tone in his voice. "I agreed to keep you up to date on my investigation. There have been some new developments."

"So I hear," he said. "That Indian was caught with Isaiah's rifle. Sort of puts everything in a new light, doesn't it?"

"I'm convinced Eagle-in-Flight had nothing to do with Holcomb's murder," Molly said, "and I think I'll be able to prove it."

Timmons glanced down the street as he reconsidered his haste in answering. "Fact is, I'm on my way to tell a good wife that her man tried to drink all the beer in The People's Choice last night, and wound up in one of my cells. I'll postpone that nasty job. Step down and come on in."

Molly swung down from the saddle and knotted the reins around the rail. She stepped up on to the boardwalk and entered Timmons' office as he pulled the door open for her. Inside she was shown to a Windsor chair beside his desk.

"I want to know everything you know," he said as he moved around his desk and sat in a swivel chair that creaked under his weight. "Can you name the murderer?"

"Not yet," Molly said, "but I believe I have the motive pinned down."

"Now, hold on," the sheriff said, leaning forward. "If you know the motive for the murders, or think you do, you must have a damned good idea who the killer is."

"I have an idea," Molly said, "but I don't have the proof to bring into a court of law."

Timmons nodded slowly as he gazed at her. "All right. Let me hear it."

Molly recounted the details of her investigation since the day she had searched Nathan Rouse's office. Timmons listened in rapt silence while she described her two trips to the Shoshone reservation, concluding with her close call at Rouse's door a quarter of an hour ago.

"You've been busy since you stepped off the train here," Timmons said, clearly impressed with the thoroughness of her investigation.

"A case like this one has many angles to it," Molly said.

"You've followed every one of them, sounds like," he said. "If I ever need an investigator, I'll come hunting for you." He paused as he reflected on all that he had just heard. "See if I have this thing straight. You figure Pardee and Rouse are trying to scare Mrs. Holcomb off because they've found gold somewhere on the Pitchfork."

Molly nodded. "But I think it goes deeper than that, sheriff. Pardee wants the ranch, and I believe he is trying to scare Nell into selling out. That's why he attacked the Shoshones. But I found correspondence in Rouse's files indicating he is recommending to the Indian Bureau in Washington that the whole tribe be moved out of the state."

"How does that fit into your theory?" Timmons asked.

"I think Rouse discovered gold on Shoshone lands," Molly said.

The sheriff's eyes widened.

"Rouse and Pardee are working together so each can get what he wants," Molly went on. "Pardee wants the Pitchfork, and Rouse wants the Shoshones shipped off the reservation so he can go in there and stake his claim."

Timmons exhaled loudly. "That's some notion you've got there, Miss Owens, some notion." He paused. "What do you think the motive for killing Isaiah Holcomb was?"

"I believe he somehow found out about the gold discovery," Molly said, "perhaps from the Shoshones, and was on his way to report it to Colonel Stobaugh."

"By God, that makes sense," Timmons said. "But what about Jack McGrath?"

"His nose for news took him to the killer," Molly said, "and that night the killer silenced him."

"So who's the murderer," Timmons asked, "Pardee or Rouse?"

Molly shrugged. "That's what I meant when I told you I had the motive pinned down but couldn't name the killer."

"How do you aim to find out?" he asked.

Molly smiled. "I'm going to become a partner."

CHAPTER XXIV

Joe Pardee was a hard-bitten man who often bullied the men who worked for him on the Pitchfork. But for all that, Molly sensed he was the weak link in the Rouse-Pardee conspiracy. He was not as smart as Rouse. He was also a heavy drinker and evidently something of a worrier.

Molly thought of this as she rode back to the ranch, and decided to make her first move.

In the middle of the afternoon Molly came out onto the veranda as Joe Pardee and a dozen cowhands came riding in from the south. She realized that after leaving Rouse's office Pardee must have ridden onto Pitchfork range and joined the men as they rounded up and herded cattle to new pasture.

She waited until the men had turned out their horses in the corral and washed up at the pump by the bunkhouse, and then she called to Pardee. He came across the yard, looking at her suspiciously.

"What do you want?" he asked, jaw clenched.

Molly came down the veranda steps. "I've been thinking about you, Joe."

"That so," he said, eyes narrowing.

She nodded, still smiling at him. "I know we've had our differences, but I've admired the way you run this outfit. Without you holding things together after Mr. Holcomb's death, the Pitchfork would be in a shambles by now."

"Could be," Pardee allowed.

"I want you to know that I hope you stay on to ramrod the outfit," Molly said. "The men respect you, and I'll need you—"

"Stay on," he repeated. "What're you driving at?"

"I want you to stay here as foreman," Molly said. "You see, Joe, there'll be some changes around here." She paused and went on in a confidential tone of voice, "You might as well hear this from me, Joe. I didn't come to the Pitchfork just to comfort Nell. I had another reason."

Pardee's eyebrows arched. "I figured that all along. What's your game?"

"No game," Molly said. "Nell and I have talked it over, and she's decided she wants to keep this ranch in the family. I'll take over the operation—"

"The hell!" Pardee exclaimed.

"I know it'll take some getting used to, Joe," Molly said.

"Nell never told me nothing about this!" he said. "She said she'd either hang on herself, or sell to me."

"She's changed her mind," Molly said, "now that she knows I'm willing to take over and handle the books and payroll and all the jobs she doesn't want to be troubled with."

"You mean, you sweet-talked your way into this ranch," Pardee said, his face darkening.

"Call it what you will, Joe," Molly said, "but from now on you'll report to me every morning."

"By God, I'll have to hear that from Mrs. Holcomb," he said, shoving past her as he leaped up the steps to the veranda. Molly watched as he crossed the porch in long strides, throwing the door open as he went in.

She waited half a minute, and then climbed the steps and entered the ranch house, pulling the door shut after her. She heard Nell confirm what she had just told Pardee.

Hands on his narrow hips, the foreman glared down at Nell who held Morning Star's baby in her arms. He cast an angry glance at Molly, then turned and stomped out of the front room through the mess hall and kitchen, slamming the outside door as he left.

"Oh, my," Nell said in a whisper. She looked up at Molly. "I hope we're not doing the wrong thing."

"We aren't," Molly said. "If he's innocent, no harm will be done. But if he's guilty—"

"I can hardly stand to think of it," Nell said. "All along Joe knew who murdered my Isaiah. . . ." Her voice trailed off and her eyes grew wet with tears as she looked down at the sleeping baby in her arms.

In the morning after breakfast Molly called Pardee into the dining room. On the table in front of her were stacks of papers, ledgers, and tally books. Nell sat in her wheelchair nearby.

"Joe, I burned the midnight oil last night while I went over these records," Molly said as the foreman stood before her, Stetson in his hands.

"Everything in order?" he asked in a neutral tone of voice.

"Seems to be," Molly replied. "I can see clearly that the Pitchfork's going broke."

"Broke," Pardee repeated. "How do you figure that?"

"Simple," Molly said pleasantly. "Too much payroll."

"Well, I've explained to Mrs. Holcomb why we're carrying so many men on the payroll now. We have to protect the herds—"

"I know that," Molly said. "But we're going to have to make some changes—quickly."

"What sort of changes?" he asked.

"We'll have to cut loose some of those men you've got riding patrol out there," Molly said.

Impatience gave his voice an edge when he said, "If we don't protect Pitchfork herds, we'll lose 'em."

"The army has increased their patrols," Molly said. "We don't need our own army now."

"Well, I reckon I could let a few cowhands go," Pardee said.

"That isn't what I had in mind, Joe," Molly said. "We'll keep all the original cowhands. Those men have worked here several seasons, and proven their worth. It's the new men I want you to cut loose—every one of them."

Pardee sputtered, and looked to Nell for help. She remained silent. Pardee swung his gaze back to Molly.

"I want you to take care of that job today, Joe," Molly said.

Pardee nodded curtly. "All right, I'll do it. But don't come crying to me when the Shoshones run prime steers off Pitchfork pasture to the reservation."

"I won't come crying to you, Joe," Molly said, meeting his gaze.

Pardee clapped his hat on his head, turned, and stomped out of the dining room.

In the morning Pardee's gunmen took their last meal in Lun Sing's mess hall. Afterwards they carried their war bags out of the bunkhouse, saddled their horses, and rode out.

Molly watched this from the dining room window. Pardee stood out there, hands on his hips above his gunbelt. He swayed slightly, and Molly realized he had started this day with a bottle.

She left the house through the front door and called to him. "Joe."

Pardee did not move, and for a long moment seemed unwilling to acknowledge her call.

"Joe, I'd like a word with you."

He turned slowly and walked unhurriedly to the steps. "What do you want now?"

Molly descended the veranda steps and met him, watching his bloodshot eyes widen in utter surprise when she held out her closed hand and opened it.

"You know what this is?" she asked, showing him an egg-sized sample of gold ore.

Pardee eyed the rock with its deep yellow cast, and then looked at her.

"It's gold, Joe," Molly said matter-of-factly. "Not pure, but as rich an outcropping as I've ever seen— even down in Cripple Creek, Colorado."

"Where . . . where'd you find that?" he asked.

"Not far from here," Molly said.

"Where, exactly?" Pardee demanded. "On Pitchfork land?"

"The location will have to be my secret for now," she said.

"You found that on Shoshone land," he said. "Didn't you?"

Molly pretended to be surprised. "You're a shrewd man, Joe."

"I knew you'd been back in that country," he said. "You might as well tell me everything."

Molly shook her head. "I can tell you there's plenty more of this yellow rock up there, enough to make us both rich, and I'm going to need help in bringing it out."

Pardee folded his arms over his chest. "Now I know why you talked Nell into staying on the ranch. You're not interested in the cattle business. You want to start a gold mine—an illegal gold mine."

"The outcropping will have to be worked quietly," Molly said.

"Can't be done," Pardee said. "You can't bust rock without making noise and muddying the water. You'll need miners and you'll need guards—plenty of them."

"Can you hire them?" Molly asked.

Pardee swore softly. "You talk smart, lady, but you sure as hell don't act smart. We had some good men right here, but you had to go and fire them." He exhaled angrily, sending out a gust of whiskey-laden breath. "You won't get a lick of help from me, lady." He turned and walked away, heading for the horse barn.

Molly returned to the ranch house. From a window there she watched the barn. Presently Pardee came out on his gray quarterhorse. He rode out through the gate at a high lope, heading for Crowheart.

CHAPTER XXV

Molly heard a vehicle roll into the yard that evening. She left her chair by the fireplace and went to a front window in time to see Nathan Rouse pull his one-horse buggy to a halt at the bottom of the veranda steps.

Molly moved to the door and opened it, seeing the Indian agent's hardened smile as he crossed the porch toward her.

"I hear you're trying to get yourself thrown in jail again," he said.

Molly did not reply, but she blocked his path at the door. A head taller, she looked down at the man as they faced one another. He was dressed the same way he'd been the first time she saw him, his bowler cocked jauntily to one side, but the resemblance ended there. His body was stiffened with anger.

"You've been searching the Shoshone reservation for minerals, haven't you?" he said. He stuck out one puffy hand. "Give me that gold sample."

"Joe Pardee wasted no time in reporting to you, did he?" Molly asked.

"He was doing his duty as a citizen," Rouse said. "We're working together to keep the peace around here."

"You can drop that pious act of yours," Molly said. "It won't work with me. I know what you and Pardee are up to."

"What the devil are you talking about?" he demanded.

"I was in the Shoshone encampment the day Pardee and his gunmen used those Indians for a turkey shoot," Molly said. "You two are working together, doing everything you can to get the Shoshones thrown out of Wyoming."

Rouse glared at her for a long moment. In a low, menacing voice, he said, "You can't prove a word of that."

"I can," Molly said, "and if I have to, I will. I know what you're hiding in your office safe."

Rouse softly cursed. "So that's where you got the gold sample."

"That's a good guess," Molly said, "and there's only one way you can guarantee my silence. I want a piece of that gold discovery."

"So you want in," he said.

Molly nodded. "As a full partner. With me running the Pitchfork, I'll earn my share. In fact, you can't swing this operation without me."

"You may think you have the upper hand," Rouse said, "but I'll be damned if I'm going to knuckle under to you."

"You've heard the deal," Molly said. "No need for us to be enemies."

He shook his head. "Not a chance, lady, not one chance in hell."

"I'll give you twenty-four hours to change your mind," Molly said. "By then you should see the wisdom of dealing me in."

With a curse, he turned away. Molly watched him descend the stairs and climb into his buggy without looking back. He whipped the horse and drove away.

A few minutes after he topped the low hill beyond the ranch gate, a lone horsebacker appeared over the top of the hill a hundred yards off the road. The rider paused there until Molly waved, and then came down the slope at an angle where he would not be seen if Rouse had looked back.

Sheriff Timmons came through the gate at a fast trot, reining up at the veranda. Molly met him at the hitching rail.

"Just like you figured," he said, "Pardee came to Rouse's office this afternoon, and then headed straight for The People's Choice. Probably still there. If ever I saw a man who looked like he was in a drinking mood, Pardee was."

Timmons went on, "I kept an eye on Rouse's office, like you said. When he got his buggy out of the Smythe Livery, I fetched my horse and followed him. Sure enough, he came storming up here, whipping his horse all the way. Looks like you've given them plenty to worry about."

"I told Rouse I'd give him twenty-four hours to let me into their scheme," Molly said.

"Think he will?" Timmons asked.

Molly nodded. "He'll let me think I'm in. Then I should be able to get the proof I need."

Timmons shook his head. "You've stirred up a hornet's nest, Miss Owens. If you're right about that pair, they've killed two men who were on to them. Likely, they won't stop at the notion of killing a woman."

In her bedroom that night Molly undressed and put on a flannel nightgown that reached to her ankles. After combing out her long blonde hair, she climbed into bed. The nights had grown increasingly chilly since her arrival, and lately she had slept under the comfortable weight of a wool blanket and two quilts.

For a time Molly lay in the cold darkness, eyes open, thinking of her investigation. Answers to her questions had led her to the principals of this case in Crowheart, the Pitchfork Ranch, Camp Lincoln, and the Shoshone reservation. Each place possessed a life of its own, and they interacted with one another to create a human fabric. That fabric of life here had been slashed by a murderer. Molly fell asleep thinking of tomorrow.

A sudden sensation of warmth awakened her, and the stench of whiskey filled her nostrils. Opening her eyes to darkness, she sensed more than saw a man standing over her, leaning down. Then she heard the oiled *click* of a revolver hammer thumbed back, and cold steel of a gun barrel pressed against her cheek.

"One sound out of you, one holler, and I'll pull the trigger."

Molly recognized the slurred voice of Joe Pardee. "What do you want?" she whispered.

"Shut up," he said, jamming the gun barrel against her face. "I want you. I'm gonna take my pleasure with you like I shoulda done the first damned night you got here. Showed you who's boss, showed you a real man, that's what I shoulda done. . . ."

"If you shoot me, you'll never get away—"

"Shut up!" Pardee said. "I can pull this trigger and leave through the window before anyone's out of bed. Now, you do what I tell you, Miss Molly Owens, and keep your damned mouth shut if you want to go on living."

Molly saw the shadowy figure of the man straighten up. "Get some clothes on. We're going for a ride. You like to go on long rides when you're snooping around, don't you? Well, that's just what we're gonna do, take us a long horseback ride."

Molly hesitated as she sat up in bed. She weighed the odds. If Pardee intended to kill her, she might just as well make her fight right here in this dark bedroom.

"Get up," Pardee said. "You like gold, don't you? You wanna see some? Well, I'll show you more gold than you ever dreamed about."

Molly swung her feet out of bed, deciding at that moment to play along with him for now.

Pardee struck a match. "I like a good show. I'm gonna watch you strip." The flame cast weird shadows on his unshaven face as he leered at her. "Make it good, but make it quick. We have to get riding."

Molly crossed the bedroom to the curtained closet along the wall opposite the bed. By the wavering light of the match she found her riding skirt. She stepped into it and just as she raised her nightgown to her thighs, the flame singed Pardee's fingers.

He cursed and let the match drop. It struck the floor and went out.

Molly pulled the skirt up and hastily took off her nightgown. She heard Pardee fumbling for another match in a vest pocket under his coat. But by the time he found one and struck it, Molly was buttoning her blouse.

"Come on," Pardee growled. He blew out the match.

In the darkness Molly heard him move to the window and open it. She pulled on her riding boots and got her coat and Stetson off the pegs in the closet.

Molly reached for her derringer. The holster hung from another peg, but before she could get it, Pardee's drunken impatience boiled over. Spurs ringing as his boots scuffed on the floor, he came for her, grasped her arm and yanked her toward the window.

Molly realized this had been his plan all along when she climbed outside and by starlight saw a pair of horses saddled and waiting. One was Pardee's gray; the other was her buckskin gelding.

By the light of stars in the black sky they rode through the timbered foothills toward the great basin at the foot of the Owl Mountains. They nearly blundered into a Shoshone camp in a small clearing, but halted in the trees before they were heard.

Pardee drew his revolver as he looked at the shadowy forms of half a dozen warriors sleeping around the embers of a dying fire. Spotted ponies were tied nearby, asleep on their feet.

"By God, I could shoot them all before they knew what hit them," he muttered.

Molly guided her horse closer to his to be in a position to hit his gun hand, but a moment later Pardee lowered the weapon and holstered it.

"Hell with it," he whispered. "Might be more of the bastards around here. Ride around them."

By frosty starlight they went on through the forest, reaching the basin at the first light of day. After resting and watering the horses, they crossed the basin at a high lope, and entered the pine forest on the other side. Pardee glanced back, and then abruptly reined up, ordering Molly to do the same.

Molly turned her horse and followed Pardee's gaze across the basin. A rider was there, alone, coming toward them through the high grass.

Molly stared, trying to determine whether the horsebacker was Indian or white. She did not see what Pardee was up to until she heard the lariat softly sing through the air.

The loop settled around her shoulders, and before she could throw it off Pardee's horse backed away, drawing it tight. With a sharp tug, Pardee jerked her out of the saddle.

Molly landed hard flat on her back. The breath rushed out of her, and she lay there, dazed.

Pardee swung down and came to her, carrying the coiled rope. He quickly looped it around her feet, rolled her over and tied her wrists together. He gagged her with his handkerchief and left her there, hog-tied.

Molly caught her breath and turned on her side. She saw Pardee move the horses back into the trees. He came out, revolver drawn, and knelt behind a thick growth of brush.

After a long wait Molly saw the rider come into the trees from the basin, intent on following the trail. Molly wanted to shout a warning as Pardee raised his revolver, but could not. The rider was Morning Star.

CHAPTER XXVI

Molly watched in horror as Morning Star rode through the trees, straight into Joe Pardee's ambush.

Crouching behind the leafy thicket, he waited, gun poised in his hand. When Morning Star came within half a dozen yards on the other side of the bushes, he abruptly stood and took aim.

"Damn you, Indian!" he said.

Alarmed, Morning Star's head snapped around, and the Pitchfork mare reared up. Morning Star spilled out of the saddle, and the mare trotted away.

"I'd shoot you right here, damn you," Pardee said, coming around the thicket, "but I can't take a chance on bringing a war party down on me. Rouse always said Indians wouldn't come back into these mountains, but I never believed it. A little superstition didn't stop you, did it?"

Molly watched Pardee as he stood over the fallen Morning Star. From here Molly could not see her, but she heard the woman crying softly and knew she was looking into Pardee's gun barrel.

"Hell," he said, holstering his revolver, "you're coming, too." He glanced at Molly. "I'll take my pleasure out of the two of you."

Molly watched as he bent down and yanked Morning Star to her feet. When the Indian woman saw her, she pulled away from Pardee and ran to her.

"Sure, go ahead and untie her," he said. "We've got a long ride in front of us, and it looks like you two will be riding double."

Pardee rode behind them as they made their way through a long canyon choked with scrubby pines. Molly saw many signs of other shod horses, and

150

realized pack trains had passed through here recently. By noon she understood why.

"All right," Pardee said, "rein up and climb off that big horse."

The canyon widened into a grassy clearing. In the middle was a huge pile of boxes and packing crates labeled "U.S. GOVERNMENT." Molly turned and looked back at Pardee.

"Rouse deprived the Indians of their government allotments," Molly said, "and you held back on the delivery of Pitchfork steers."

"Shut up," Pardee said, moving his hand to his gun butt, "and climb down."

"You had a pretty good plan," Molly said as she swung down from the saddle, "for stirring up the Indians. What I don't understand is why you attacked the Shoshone encampment that morning?"

Pardee scowled. "Because of you."

"Me?" Molly said in surprise. "Because I was in the encampment?"

"No," Pardee said, "we never knew you were there. All we wanted to do was speed things up some. The Indians would have attacked the Pitchfork or Crowheart after they got hungry enough, but we knew you had ideas of taking over the ranch. I told Rouse you wouldn't scare."

"So you tried to scare Nell into signing the ranch over to you," Molly said.

"Hell, it'll be best for her anyway," he said. "She can't run that cattle ranch from a wheelchair."

"That's for her to decide, isn't it?" Molly asked.

"By God, I'm going to enjoy having my way with you, woman," he said, moving toward her. The whiskey had worn off, but the long ride and lack of sleep had left him tired and haggard in the face.

Molly wanted to keep him talking. "You planned to buy the ranch with gold, didn't you? Just where is this mine?"

"It's where I'm taking you," Pardee said, drawing his gun. "Over that way."

Molly looked around as he motioned with the gun barrel toward a stand of aspens. A well-traveled footpath led through the grass. She turned and walked to the aspen grove, and Morning Star followed.

Entering the cool shadows of the trees, Molly peered through the branches of fluttering leaves and saw a granite outcropping ahead. Twice the size of a barn, the outcropping was surrounded on the mountainside by brush and trees.

The "mine" she saw as she stepped out of the aspens was little more than a shallow cavity in the gray granite, a cavity that had been chiseled out by men working with single jacks. Their tools, along with empty tins of food and discarded packages of chewing tobacco, lay scattered in the loose rock at the base of the outcropping.

Molly moved closer to it, seeing yellow ore in the stone. *A prospector's dream*, she thought, as she examined the ore body. The wide vein of pure gold was worth a fortune.

Molly glanced over her shoulder at Pardee. He stared at the gold as though transfixed by the sight.

"Rouse found this?" Molly asked.

Pardee blinked and nodded. "A Shoshone medicine man told him about it last year, and Rouse finally talked the old boy into showing it to him."

"And you've been working it ever since," Molly said, "bringing ore out by night in pack trains."

Pardee nodded again, his expression turning angry. "Until you fired the men we brought in to do the job."

"You couldn't have kept it secret for long," Molly said. "Gold makes men talk."

"We'd have kept the secret long enough to get the Indians out of here," Pardee said. "The men we hired were well paid, and they knew nobody would get anything if they talked." He glared at her. "You did your best to ruin everything we built."

"I'm not the only one," Molly said. "Isaiah Holcomb found out what you and Rouse were up to. That's why you had to put a knife in him."

"Damn you," Pardee said in a low voice, "I never harmed him. I couldn't. He hired me when I was nothing but an overgrown boy."

"Then how did it happen?" Molly asked.

"I'm not telling you a damn thing," he said. "Now, get over here in the grass and take off your clothes. Come on, both of you."

Molly wanted to keep him talking. She moved slowly toward a patch of grass at the edge of the aspen grove. "I wish I could believe you, Joe. But I know Isaiah Holcomb didn't leave you any choice. Once he found out about the gold—"

"Damn you," Pardee said, "you think you know everything. You don't have no idea what happened. . . ."

Molly heard his voice crack with fatigue and anger. "Then tell me the truth so I will know," she said.

"Isaiah found out, all right," Pardee said, "from the same medicine man who brought Rouse up here. Isaiah didn't know I was in the deal. See, I was just gonna help Rouse get the gold off reservation land, that's all. But after Isaiah found out, he told me he was gonna ride for Camp Lincoln."

"So you got word to Rouse?" Molly said.

Pardee nodded. "I figured somehow he could talk Isaiah out of reporting it to Stobaugh." His face twisted with anguish. "The next thing I know, Isaiah's body was brought in. Hell, I was tore up about it like everybody else."

He drew a breath. "I never figured Rouse would go that far. But that night when he came to pay his respects to Nell, he took me outside and told me the Pitchfork could be mine if I played it right. At first I wanted nothing to do with the deal. But after Rouse explained things to me, I figured he was right. What was done was done, and there wasn't no backing up.

Nell would sell off the ranch one day, and I'd be left high and dry. I might as well be the man to take over." Pardee added with conviction, "I never killed Isaiah. That's the truth. I had nothing to do with it."

"Nothing but switching your loyalty from the man who gave you your start in life to a man who promised to make you rich," Molly said.

"By God!" Pardee shouted hoarsely. He rushed to her, raising his revolver. "I'm gonna pistol-whip you until you can't use that damned mouth of yours."

In the moment he came lunging for her, Pardee's attention left Morning Star. The Indian woman ran toward him, her moccasined feet padding heavily in the grass.

Pardee heard her or caught a glimpse of movement. He paused in his attack and half-turned, but had no time to either dodge or take aim. The stout Morning Star butted her head into his chest, bowling him over.

Pardee grunted when he went down. He sprawled in the grass, but held on to his gun. Molly watched in horror as Morning Star fell beside him, rolling away to come up on all fours while Pardee leveled his revolver at her and drew back the hammer.

Molly quickly closed the distance between them, drawing one foot back. She kicked Pardee's wrist. He yelled in pain as the big Colt .45 looped into the air end over end, landing in the tall grass twenty feet away.

"You busted my hand!" he screamed. He raised up on his knees and clenched his wrist, rocking back and forth.

While Morning Star backed away from him, Molly ran through the grass and picked up his revolver. She came back to the kneeling Pardee and aimed the gun point-blank between his eyes.

Pardee stared at her, his pained expression turning fearful. "What . . . what you gonna do?"

"Shoot you," Molly said matter-of-factly, "just like you planned to do to us."

Pardee shook his head, not taking his eyes from the gun barrel inches away from his face. "I wasn't gonna kill you . . . just figured on scaring you."

Molly shifted the barrel to one side and pulled the trigger.

The shot shattered the wilderness silence, and left Molly's ears ringing. The bullet had missed Pardee's head by a fraction of an inch, singeing his skin with a powder burn.

Pardee bowed his head. His shoulders heaved as he was wracked by sobs.

"You have one chance to ride out of here alive," Molly said. "Just one. Tell me the truth."

"I told . . . told you . . . truth." He raised up, looking at her with a pleading expression. "I swear, I swear to God."

Molly cocked the revolver again and aimed it between his eyes. "Who killed Jack McGrath?"

"Rouse knifed him, too," Pardee said, relieved. "That's the truth. I had nothing to do with it."

"Sure, you're a victim of circumstances," Molly said.

Pardee's face hardened. "I never killed anyone."

Molly motioned for him to stand. "I'm going to give you an opportunity to do the right thing, Pardee."

He stared at her. "What?"

"Testify against Nathan Rouse," Molly said.

Pardee's expression was unchanged as he looked up at Molly.

"If you don't," she said, "you'll hang for murders he committed. Now, get on your feet."

Molly held Pardee at gunpoint as they walked back through the aspen grove to the horses. She mounted, and Morning Star swung up behind her. Then Molly ordered Pardee to mount his horse.

"Lead the way," she said, "and don't forget—I'm right behind you."

Pardee grabbed his saddle horn with his good hand, and pulled himself up into the saddle of his gray.

Molly followed him out of the long canyon to the basin. He rode with his head bowed until they reached open ground. His quarterhorse abruptly stopped, and Pardee's head snapped up. He looked back at Molly, his face stretched in fear.

When she rode out of the trees, she saw that a Shoshone war party awaited them, probably drawn here by the gunshot. The eight warriors, armed and painted for combat, were led by Elk Bull.

CHAPTER XXVII

The warriors closed in, taking the reins of both horses. One Shoshone snatched the revolver from Molly's hand.

Elk Bull brought his pony around and began berating Pardee. Molly did not understand a word, but his tone of voice and gestures were unmistakable. He was formally accusing Pardee of a crime committed against the Shoshone people.

Morning Star confirmed this by whispering into Molly's ear. Elk Bull was recounting the attack by Pardee and his gunmen on the Shoshone village. When the whites fell back, the Indians had given chase. Elk Bull had ridden close enough that day to recognize Pardee and his gray horse. One of the old women shot down that morning was Elk Bull's mother. She died.

Without warning, Elk Bull abruptly swung his rusty rifle around and aimed at Pardee's chest. He drew the hammer back. At the sound of the dry *click*, Pardee's shoulders drew together and his body shuddered.

"No! No!" he shouted.

Elk Bull pulled the trigger. But instead of a thunderous explosion came only a soft *click*.

Elk Bull's expression showed brief surprise as he looked at the old weapon in his hands. He thumbed the hammer to cocked position again, looked angrily at Pardee as he aimed, and pulled the trigger.

Pardee's scream drowned out the *click* of the misfiring weapon. Elk Bull tried again, and the third failed attempt left Pardee wracked with hysterical laughter.

"Stop!" Molly shouted. The warrior holding the reins to her gelding tightened his grip and pulled the horse away.

Molly turned her head and saw that Elk Bull had handed the rifle to a warrior beside him, then took his bow and an arrow from the warrior's quiver.

Molly watched in horror as Elk Bull's experienced hands drew back the bow string, bending the bow to the full length of the flint-tipped arrow. He aimed at Pardee's heaving chest, and released the arrow.

Pardee's high-pitched laughter was immediately silenced. He slumped forward in the saddle. One foot came out of the stirrup, and he slid to the ground. He lay still at his horse's feet.

Even as the shock of what Molly had witnessed made her dizzy with horror and grief, she thought that it was not so much a murder as an execution. *Your life for the lives you took* was the unspoken message of this Shoshone warrior.

Elk Bull returned the bow to the warrior at his side, and then spoke to Molly. When he finished, Morning Star translated.

"He remembers the day you helped drive the white killers away from his village," she said. "Elk Bull thanks you."

The Indians turned their horses and rode away, following the tree line at the edge of the basin.

At nightfall Molly was challenged by a guard on Camp Lincoln's perimeter. She identified herself, and rode onto the parade ground. A crowd of troopers quickly gathered. By the light of lanterns they examined the body of Pardee slung across the saddle of his iron gray quarterhorse.

In his office Colonel Stobaugh listened intently while Molly described what had happened to her in the last twenty-four hours. He leaned to one side in his chair, taking weight off his injured leg.

"Miss Owens," he said, "if I didn't know something of your capabilities, I would not believe a word of what you just told me." He shook his head as he grinned.

"You'll find the government supplies just where I told you," she said.

"I have no doubt of that," he said. "You're quite a woman, Miss Owens, quite a woman." He paused. "Now the question is, what to do about Nathan Rouse."

"I'll have him arrested," Molly replied, "and charged with the murders of Isaiah Holcomb and Jack McGrath."

Stobaugh studied her. "Seems to me that you lost your best witness with the death of Joe Pardee."

"I thought about that all the way back from the reservation," Molly said, "and I have a plan. But I'll need your help."

"I'm at your service, Miss Owens," he said, "and not just because of army orders now. I want to see this thing through to the end."

Molly stood and held out her hand. "Thank you, colonel."

He got to his feet, leaning on his good leg, and shook hands with her. "I'll get you a hot supper. Tonight you can bunk in the visitors' quarters again." He added, "I'll have a tub and hot water brought in there, too."

"I know it isn't customary to allow Indians in the camp, colonel," Molly said, "but I want Morning Star to stay with me—"

"I'll make an exception for her," Stobaugh said with a wave of his hand. "An extra plate will be set at the officers' table, and another bunk will be made up in your quarters."

In the morning Molly watched from the plank porch of HQ as Stobaugh sent out a detachment of troopers to the reservation. A string of pack animals went with them. The troopers carried a white flag, and their assignment was to locate and bring back the store of supplies Molly had found in the canyon. Over breakfast Colonel Stobaugh had told her that he would turn his Shoshone prisoners loose and give out all the food, blankets, and utensils in the hidden cache.

"That should help rebuild the peace around here," Stobaugh said.

"What will happen to Elk Bull?" Molly asked.

"I want a written report from you that I can forward to Fort Robinson," Stobaugh said. "If the army still wants him brought in, I'll make the effort." He paused. "But that Indian may be hard to find."

Molly looked across the mess table at him and saw a faint smile on his lips.

CHAPTER XXVIII

Molly reached Crowheart before noon. After stopping off at the jailhouse, she rode to the Indian Bureau office. She climbed the staircase and opened the door without knocking.

Nathan Rouse looked up from his desk, his eyes widening in amazement.

"Next time you want a job done right," Molly said, "do it yourself."

"What are you talking about?" Rouse demanded.

"You know what I'm talking about," Molly said. "After you left Pitchfork, you came back here and pulled Pardee out of The People's Choice. You should have sobered him up before you sent him after me. Maybe then he'd have left me at the mine the way you told him to."

"Miss Owens," Rouse said, "I don't have the slightest notion of what you're talking about."

"Playing innocent won't help you now," Molly said. "I know everything."

He leaned back in his chair, regarding her. "All right, just what do you know, or think you know?"

"I know you murdered Isaiah Holcomb," Molly said, "and I know why. Pardee warned you that Holcomb had found out about the gold discovery and would report it to Colonel Stobaugh the next day. You were waiting for him in that little meadow, weren't you, armed with a new trade knife?"

"Get out of my office," Rouse said.

"Joe Pardee told me the whole story," she went on. "It's all over. You'll hang for Holcomb's murder—and for the murder of Jack McGrath."

Rouse slapped a hand down on the desk top and stood, glaring at her.

"Jack came to you that day you had me jailed, didn't he?" Molly asked. "He came to you and confronted you with some facts that must have surprised you. He was close enough to the truth that you knew you had to do away with him—"

"You can't prove a word of what you're saying," Rouse said in a low voice.

"I can," Molly said, "with Joe Pardee's testimony."

A cherubic smile came to the Indian agent's mouth. "My word against his. It was all his doing—the gold mine, everything."

"But you hired the gunmen," Molly said, "and you hired the men to use the single jacks and pack the ore off the reservation. You can bet I'll get testimony out of them, too."

Rouse glared at her. "That doesn't make me a murderer."

"So you're an innocent man," Molly said.

"That's right," Rouse said. "Now get out."

Molly turned and went to the door. She stepped out on the landing and gestured toward the bottom of the staircase.

"What the hell—" Rouse began, moving toward her.

Molly stepped back into the office, blocking Rouse's way. In a moment Colonel Stobaugh came up the stairs. He was followed by Sheriff Timmons. The two men entered the office.

"What's going on here?" Rouse demanded, his gaze darting from one face to another.

No one spoke until the last two people climbed the staircase and moved silently inside. Morning Star was followed by Eagle-in-Flight.

With Morning Star translating, Molly asked the Shoshone chieftain, "Did you see the murder of Isaiah Holcomb?"

Eagle-in-Flight nodded. He stared at Nathan Rouse.

"Is the killer in this room?" Molly asked.

Eagle-in-Flight listened to Morning Star, and nodded again.

"Who is he?" Molly asked.

Eagle-in-Flight raised his arm and pointed to the Indian agent.

"This is absurd," Rouse said with a forced laugh. "That stinking savage had Holcomb's rifle. He's the killer, and he's accusing me to protect himself."

"That story might hold water," Molly said, "except for one thing."

"What?" Rouse demanded.

"You confessed to Joe Pardee," Molly said, "and he's ready to testify in court. He didn't kill Isaiah Holcomb, and he's not planning to take the blame for you. He'll tell the whole story of how you came to him with the idea of scaring Nell Holcomb and then buying the Pitchfork with gold mined on the Shoshone reservation. And that was only the beginning. You broke the peace between whites and Indians and nearly started a small war—all because you had found gold on reservation land."

Rouse's face reddened as he glared at Molly.

Sheriff Timmons stepped forward. "You're under arrest, Rouse."

In the next instant Nathan Rouse lunged behind Molly and grabbed her. Molly was nearly jerked off her feet when she was pulled back against him. His free hand came out from under his coat, and Molly caught a glimpse of polished steel as a long-bladed knife was pressed against her chest.

"Damn you!" Rouse shouted, breathing hard. "I had a right to that gold! The savages wouldn't have done anything with it. Nobody's going to take it away from me!"

Molly felt his panicked grasp and saw the others standing frozen in shocked silence. Timmons' hand rested on his gun butt, and Stobaugh's face was set in anger. Molly looked down at the blade of the trade knife pressed against her chest.

She tried to distract Rouse with a question. "Not even Isaiah Holcomb?"

"That's right!" Rouse exclaimed. "Not even that self-righteous bastard. He thought his word was law around here. Well, I showed him!"

Rouse took a ragged breath. "Now, get out of here—all of you. Get out, or I'll cut this woman open!"

"You'll never get out of here," Sheriff Timmons said. "Drop the knife and let her go—"

"Shut up!" Rouse said. "Do what I told you. Get out! Go on!" In his passion Rouse waved the knife at them.

Molly saw her chance. She brought her hands up and grasped his wrist. In a brief struggle, Rouse tried to pull the knife back and stab her.

Molly kicked his shin with one foot and when he cried out, she shoved his knife hand up, stepped under it, and gave his arm a sudden downward thrust, twisting his wrist. The knife clattered to the floor, and Rouse's feet became airborne. He went head over heels, landing with a *thud* flat on his back.

Timmons rushed to the prone figure of the Indian agent, drawing his revolver. Stobaugh limped across the office and picked up the trade knife. Morning Star came to Molly and embraced her.

Rouse was too dazed to resist as Timmons hand-cuffed him and pulled him to his feet.

"I do believe," Stobaugh said, "that of all the people in this room Rouse could have grabbed, he picked the wrong one."

"I know what you've told me is true," Nell said, "but I still can't believe it." She spoke those words as she stood on the veranda of the ranch house, supporting her weight on her good leg and a cane loaned to her by Bud.

Molly and Morning Star stood beside her, and at the base of the steps Sheriff Timmons held the reins of his horse.

"My Isaiah treated Joe like a son," Nell went on, "from the day he came here looking as gaunt as a lost steer." She paused. "That was a long time ago."

Molly said, "Joe Pardee didn't like what he was doing. He used whiskey to help him forget. On that day he warned Rouse your husband would ride to Camp Lincoln, I don't think he knew what the result would be."

Nell nodded, and then turned to Morning Star as her baby whimpered. Morning Star held the infant in her arms, gently rocking him.

"He's probably looking for his 'grandma,' " Nell said with a smile.

Sheriff Timmons swung into his saddle. "I'd better ride for town."

"Thanks for escorting me to the Pitchfork," Molly said.

"I'm the one who ought to be thanking you, Miss Owens," Timmons said. "Folks are giving me more credit than I deserve for bringing Rouse in. I arrested him, but you're the one who caught him. You had the idea of making him think Pardee was still alive and ready to testify, and you broke him by piling up the evidence."

Molly asked, "Will you run for reelection, sheriff?"

"I'm thinking on it," he replied. "Folks are suddenly worried I might not, and everybody's real friendly." He paused. "People are fickle, aren't they?"

Timmons raised a hand in a farewell wave, and turned his horse.

Nell watched him ride out through the ranch gate, and turned to Molly. "Now, there's no need for you to be in such a hurry to go. You told me you wired your final report to New York City, so Zachary will soon know you did the job he wanted done. I'll write to him and tell him I've decided to keep the Pitchfork for as long as I've got a breath in my body."

"I'm glad to hear that, Nell," Molly said.

"With Morning Star and Lun Sing helping me," she said, "and with the help of Bud and all the cowhands, I should be able to turn a profit this year just like Isaiah would have wanted." She added, "Now, I want you to stay here for a good long visit, a peaceful one this time."

Molly smiled. "I have a ticket on the passenger train that comes through day after tomorrow."

"And you're dead set on that?" Nell asked.

Molly nodded.

"Well, I figured as much," Nell said. "That's why your dinner's tomorrow evening."

"Dinner?" Molly asked.

Nell grinned. "For once I'm ahead of you, aren't I? We're having a big dinner in your honor. Everybody will be here, all the cowhands, folks from town that you know, Camp Lincoln, and who knows, maybe even a few Shoshones from the reservation will ride in. We've slaughtered three steers, and I've put the word out that we're having a big feed in your honor."

"Nell," Molly said, "I wouldn't miss that for the world."

Stephen Overholser was born in Bend, Oregon, the middle son of Western author, Wayne D. Overholser. Convinced, in his words, that "there was more to learn outside of school than inside," he left Colorado State College in his senior year. He was drafted and served in the U.S. Army in Vietnam. Following his discharge, he launched his career as a writer, publishing three short stories in *Zane Grey Western Magazine*. On a research visit to the University of Wyoming at Laramie, he came across an account of a shocking incident that preceded the Johnson County War in Wyoming in 1892. It was this incident that became the inspiration for his first novel, *A Hanging at Sweetwater* (1974), that received the Spur Award from the Western Writers of America. *Molly and the Confidence Man* (1975) followed, the first in a series of books about Molly Owens, a clever, resourceful, and tough undercover operative working for a fictional detective agency in the Old West. Among the most notable of Stephen Overholser's later titles are *Search for the Fox* (1976) and *Track of a Killer* (1982). Stephen Overholser's latest novel is *Dark Embers at Dawn*.